Curse

of the

Komodo

To Trace
Best Wishes!
M. C. Berkhousen

Curse of the Komodo

M.C. Berkhousen

Illustrations by Kalpart

RISING PHOENIX PRESS

Text Copyright © 2017 Margaret C. Berkhousen

All rights reserved.
Published 2017 by Progressive Rising Phoenix Press, LLC
www.progressiverisingphoenix.com

ISBN: 978-1-946329-39-4

Printed in the U.S.A.
1st Printing

Book & Cover Design by Kalpart.
Visit www.kalpart.com

Front Cover illustration by Kalpart.

For Connor and Evan Muse

Acknowledgements

I'd like to thank Amanda M. Thrasher and Progressive Rising Phoenix Press for their help in publishing this book. Thanks also to my supportive and helpful editor, Kathleen Marusak. Thank you Tim Herman, MS., Herpetologist, for providing information about reptiles and zoo procedures; any errors are my own. A big thank you to Connor Muse for a wealth of animal information and assistance with plot points; to Evan Muse who read an early draft and cheered me on, and to Jennifer Muse for reviewing the manuscript and providing ongoing encouragement. Thanks to Maxwell Kelso for his review of the manuscript and helpful feedback. Thanks to my writing critique partners: Pamela Kelso, Judith Scharren, Joette Rozanski, also the late Christine Holliday and the late Eileen Towse. Profound thanks to my beloved children, Amy, Jennifer and David, who gave me the heart to write, and to family and friends who always believed I could do it.

Table of Contents

Chapter One—Cursed

Blood dripped from Austin's nose. Gramps shoved himself up from his chair and stared at me.

"What's the matter with you, Luke? You hurt Austin. How could you do that?"

"He started it, Gramps." I glared at my brother. "He's always bothering me."

"I didn't hit him," yelled Austin. "But he hit me, hard!" He brushed tears from his eyes then bolted up the stairs.

"I'm sick of all this fighting. You both are too old for this." Gramps plopped down again in the chair. His face was red and he was breathing hard.

Gramps stabbed a finger at me. "When Austin comes down, I want you to tell him you're sorry. And there will be no screens for the whole weekend. No TV and no computer games."

No TV? My favorite shows were on tonight.

"That's not fair, Gramps," I cried. "I didn't mean to hurt him."

"But you did hurt him. This has to stop." He closed his eyes and leaned his head back against the chair. "I packed your lunches."

I bit my lip. There was no point in arguing. Gramps was in charge while our folks were on vacation. Maybe he'd forget about the "no screens" by the time I got home from school.

"Did you sign the consent for the field trip, Gramps? We're going to the zoo today."

He pointed toward the kitchen. "On the counter, next to the lunches."

"Thanks." I found the paper and stuffed it into my backpack along with my lunch.

Austin thumped down the stairs. I licked my lips and tried to apologize.

"I'm sor—"

He didn't let me finish. Shoving past me, he grabbed his backpack and stamped out the front door. I followed him. Austin jumped into the car and locked the doors. I banged on the window, but he ignored me. Gramps clicked the key fob and opened the door so I could climb in.

"You forgot something, buddy." He leaned over the seat to hand Austin his lunch and the consent form. "You might need this if you want to go to the zoo today."

Austin took the form. He rubbed his eyes with the back of his hand. His cheeks were wet from crying and his nose was still bleeding. Gramps handed him a tissue.

Nobody talked on the way to school. Austin leaned his head against the window. He always did that when he was sad. He rubbed his eyes again, but the tears kept coming. I felt really bad. I wished I could take it back and start the morning over.

"One of these days you boys will realize it's nice to have a brother," said Gramps.

"I'd rather have a grizzly bear," I muttered.

"I'd rather have a Komodo dragon than you," shouted Austin. "They smell better."

He wiped his eyes again and rested his head on the window.

"Enough already. I'm not sure I can stand another week of this." Gramps eyed us through the rearview mirror. "You two act like you belong in a zoo. Maybe I'll call and see if they'll keep you there."

2

When we got to school, Austin jumped out of the car without saying goodbye to Gramps. He ran across the schoolyard and disappeared into a mob of kids.

"He forgot his lunch sack." Gramps held it out to me.

"Too bad." I slid my arms into my backpack. "I guess he won't eat today."

Gramps frowned. "Just because you have red hair is no excuse for that temper, Luke. You act like you don't even like your brother."

"I don't."

"Why not?"

"Because he won't leave me alone. He's always hanging around and butting into my business."

That was how the fight started this morning. I was reading my Nature magazine and he was reading over my shoulder. He reached over and turned a page before I finished. He was trying to show me how much faster he reads. I'd swung my fist up and backwards. I wasn't trying to hit his face. I wasn't trying to hit him at all. I just wanted him to stop breathing down my neck.

"Luke." Gramps shook his head. "Don't you understand? Austin looks up to you. That's why he's always trying to get your attention."

Yeah, right. Austin was president of my fan club.

"Whatever. I've got to get going." I started to walk away. Then I stopped. Austin was so upset he didn't eat breakfast. Now he wouldn't have lunch, either. I might not like him, but I didn't want him to go hungry. I trudged back to the car.

Gramps smiled. He reached over and handed me the brown bag. I closed the car door and headed into school.

The halls were packed with kids. I had to find Austin and give him his lunch before I went to class. The sixth-grade classes were on the lower level. As I went down the steps, I heard somebody yelling.

"Leave me alone!" It was Austin's voice.

3

I raced around the corner and saw him, but I was too far away to help. A kid named Jerry Magee had his arms around Austin's chest. He was trying to shove Austin into his locker. Austin had his feet braced against the wall. Jerry hit him in the knee and Austin crumpled to the ground.

I rammed into Magee and knocked him sideways. "Leave him alone, you big jerk," I shouted. "Pick on somebody your own size."

Jerry pulled himself back to his feet. His eyes bugged out and he was breathing hard. "Mommy's little baby needs his big brother to protect him." He jabbed his finger at Austin. "See you later, punk." He straightened his sweater and stalked off.

"Thanks for nothing." Austin got up from the floor. "Now he'll beat me up even worse."

When Jerry was out of sight, I turned back to my brother. "Why did you take that? You could have knocked him on his butt."

Austin held up his hands. "For self-defense only, remember?"

I remembered. Our Karate instructor had drilled it into us for a year.

"You can't just let him beat you up, Austin. How long has this been going on?"

"None of your business." Austin picked up his backpack and disappeared down the hall.

"Here's your lunch," I called after him. He didn't answer, and he didn't come back for it.

I stuffed his lunch bag into my backpack and headed up the stairs. The scene with Jerry bothered me. Austin could have taken him down in three seconds. He was good at Karate. He'd have at least a brown belt by now if he'd kept taking lessons. He quit because he didn't want to hurt anyone. I quit because I didn't want to get killed.

The intercom crackled as I slid into my seat. The principal read the day's announcements. The buses would leave for the zoo at nine-thirty and return home at three. We should keep together and meet in the pavilion at noon for lunch. Boy Scouts working on their nature badges were to answer the questions on the worksheets.

"Have a great time at the zoo," said the principal. The intercom crackled as she signed off.

In science class, the teacher handed back our exams. I was happy to see a big red "A" on my paper. It would probably be the only good grade I got all year.

Austin was a straight-A student. It wasn't his fault, but I hated it. Austin takes after my grandfather, who teaches physics and astronomy at the college in our town. Gramps knows lots of things. Sometimes he uses big words I can't understand. He'd be glad I aced this test, because he likes science, too. Maybe he'd give me back the screen time he took away this morning.

After first hour, I took the two lunch sacks and my consent form from my backpack and went outside to line up for the bus. I was already hungry and it wasn't anywhere near lunchtime. Austin would be hungry, too. Gramps hadn't given us our allowance, so Austin couldn't buy his lunch, either. As soon as we arrived, I'd find him and give him his lunch.

Yellow school buses from every school in the county packed the zoo parking lot. Kids poured out of the buses and flowed through the zoo's entrance gate. I watched for Austin, but it was like trying to find a raisin in a river of M&Ms. I decided to look for him later, when the crowd had thinned. I'd probably find him at the grizzly bear exhibit. Grizzlies were his favorites.

I showed my pass to the lady in the ticket booth and went straight to the Reptile House. I wanted to get there before it was too crowded. I could find Austin later.

My first stop was the snake displays. My favorite is the large glass aquarium where the cobras live. It's a cozy home for cobras. They can curl up on rocks and crawl into hollow logs, just like they do in the wild. It even rains in their glass home. As

5

usual, the cobras were asleep in the back corner, nestled behind a pile of twigs and leaves.

I stopped to check out the venomous snakes that are found in our state. I wanted Austin to see them, too. Austin got straight A's at school, but he couldn't tell a rattler from a garter snake. I'd been able to identify venomous snakes since I was six years old. I'd always known a lot about animals. Without even trying, I remembered everything I read about them. Too bad I couldn't do the same with math and history. Or Spanish. Or English.

I visited the turtles and the poisonous dart frogs, and then headed for the crocodile pit. On the way I spotted something new. It was a really big glass enclosure, much bigger than the cobra exhibit. It was almost as big as our garage at home. In the middle of the big glass pen was a huge gray lizard. It was the biggest lizard I'd ever seen—at least ten feet long. It narrowed its yellow eyes and flicked its forked yellow tongue at me. It was a Komodo dragon!

A volunteer stood near the enclosure, talking to a group of people. "This is our new exhibit." She waved her hand toward the big lizard. "It's a Komodo dragon."

I'd read about Komodo dragons, so I knew something about them. They can run twelve miles an hour or sometimes even faster. They can stand on their hind legs to reach prey in trees. They hunt water buffalo and can eat a goat whole. They eat humans, too. Their venom is poisonous and people can die from their bites.

"Their venom is poisonous," said the volunteer, "and people can die from their bites." It was like she was reading my mind.

The Komodo stared at me with dark, empty eyes. He flicked his fork tongue again and again. He looked like he wanted to come through the glass and eat me for lunch. A Komodo dragon can devour a deer in two bites. He could probably swallow me whole. Last month I read about a Komodo that walked into a Ranger station and ate the Ranger. Cold shivers went down my back. I took a deep breath. The zoo was careful about safety. The Komodo couldn't get out of that glass aquarium. Probably.

The volunteer continued. "This enclosure has two sections. There is an indoor section and an outdoor section." She pointed to the far end of the Komodo's glass enclosure. Part of it was on the outside of the building, like a little porch. The Komodo could crawl out to his porch to see grass and trees. He could look up at the sky through the glass ceiling. I was glad the Komodo had a glassed-in porch. Komodos need sunlight.

"The Komodo dragon needs a daily dose of sunlight to keep him healthy," said the volunteer. "He likes to bask in the sun."

I moved back to let the little kids get closer to the glass. Austin's class was in the group behind me, staring at the snakes. Austin was leaning his head against the glass of the cobra enclosure. He was probably sad because he was hungry. I was glad I'd brought his lunch.

Austin's group moved toward the Komodo. I waved to get his attention, holding up his lunch with my other hand. When Austin saw me, he turned and ran from the Reptile House. I went after him. He needed to stay with his class. He didn't know the zoo as well as I did, and I didn't want him getting lost.

Outside, the sky had turned a funny shade of green. The air was damp and heavy. It felt like something terrible was going to happen. It might be a bad storm, with thunder and lightning. It might even be a tornado.

The wind whistled through the trees, bending and snapping the twigs. The sky was starting to turn purple. Goosebumps prickled my skin and crept along my spine like a centipede. Where was my brother? I couldn't see him anywhere.

"Austin! Austin, where are you?" The wind roared, blowing my words away. I called Austin's name again, but he didn't answer. My mouth went dry, and something clenched in my stomach. I might not like him, but I didn't want him to get hurt.

7

Thunder crashed over my head! ZING! A bolt of lightning struck the zoo's water tower. Leaves, papers and twigs danced in the air. Colors bloomed in the graying sky, splashing it with green and blue and yellow patches. Dirt blew into my eyes. I put my hand up to keep twigs from hitting my face. A gust of wind slammed into my chest, pushing me backwards. I grabbed the rail near the outdoor section of the Komodo pen and hung on.

The wind tipped over one of the gift shop carts. Stuffed tigers and elephants rolled across the sidewalk. Stuffed pandas and monkeys caught on the bushes. A plastic possum hung from a tree branch. Or was it real? A large elephant balloon soared past me and landed on the Aviary.

The woman who ran the hot dog stand was trying to save her food. Hot dogs and buns slid out of her arms. Ketchup and mustard bottles tumbled to the ground and rolled around, streaking the pavement with yellow and red. A big zoo map crashed to the ground, but the sound was lost in the roar of the wind. Everywhere around me, people were screaming and crying out for help.

Things were falling out of the sky. A sharp twig hit me in the face. I wanted to push it away, but I didn't dare let go of the rail. Something cracked over my head. A tree limb landed next to me, brushing leaves and branches against my arms.

Where was my brother? I hoped he was inside a building. He could get hurt out here. I couldn't wait any longer. Somehow, I had to get to him. I let go of the rail and dropped to the ground.

"Austin! Austin, where are you?" The wind was so loud I couldn't hear my own voice. Trees bent and swayed. A bird fell out of the sky and landed next to me. I staggered to my feet and grabbed the rail again.

"Help! Luke! Help me!" My brother's voice screamed with the wind. I looked around, but I couldn't see him. Where was he? Squinting, I scanned the area again.

Then I saw him! Austin was in front of the grizzly bear cage, holding the rail with both hands. His legs were straight out behind him, twisting in the wind. One of his shoes was gone. He was having a hard time holding on. I had to reach him before the wind blew him away.

The Komodo was now in his outdoor pen. He paced as he moved his head from side to side, flicking his yellow forked tongue. Hand over hand, I moved along the rail surrounding the Komodo's glass enclosure. The bear cage was just across the lane. When I reached the end of the rail, I'd let go. Then I'd run across the lane and rescue my brother.

The green and yellow sky closed in around me. It bloomed pink and purple then all the colors of the rainbow. The colors began to spin like a rainbow tornado. My body whipped around in the wind, and it took all my strength to hang onto the rail. Austin wasn't as strong as I was. What would happen to him? I had to help him, fast.

The colors in the sky became shapes. They blurred and danced in the air, like something out of a nightmare. A silver cloud stretched into the shape of a huge lizard. The lizard's eyes gleamed like yellow moons. Its yellow forked tongue sent bolts of lightning across the sky. The lightning crashed and burrowed into the ground. The lizard followed the lightning and melted into a puddle next to me.

The puddle turned brown and began to bubble. It grew into the shape of a huge brown bear. The bear exploded into the sky. It pawed the darkness, shaping the air into a Silverback gorilla and then into a small red snake. In seconds they melted into a gray mist.

Everything sizzled and popped. It was like being in a giant frying pan. Animals snorted and growled. People screamed and cried. I heard Austin scream again. Fear stabbed my heart. I tried to run toward the screams, but my legs wouldn't move.

An inky fog oozed over the zoo. The sizzling stopped. The air grew lighter. I took a deep breath and sucked fresh air into my lungs. The inky black faded away, and I could see again.

I must have fallen, because the ground was damp and cold under my face. I tried to stand, but my body flopped like a wet mattress. There was something strange on the ground in front of me. It looked like a dead rabbit.

"Austin! Where are you?" He didn't answer. I couldn't see him anywhere.

My heart thudded against my ribs. I was so scared I could hardly breathe. I was three years older and thirty pounds heavier than Austin. The terrible wind had knocked me to the ground. What had it done to Austin? Maybe it blew him into the hippo pond. Maybe it took him over a moat and into the lion enclosure. The zoo was full of dangerous animals. If the wind blew Austin into one of their spaces, he'd be in big trouble. I had to find him, fast.

First, I had to figure out where I was. Nothing looked familiar. I tried to think. When the storm started, I was just outside the Reptile House. I'd been looking at the outside section of the Komodo's glass pen. Now I was inside the Reptile House, but it didn't look the same. The doors and windows were high and out of my reach. So were the snake and frog aquariums. It was like being in one of those fun houses at the fair.

Beneath me the cement was cold and damp. It smelled bad, like pee and poop and rotten rabbit guts. The Komodo stared at me, flicking its forked yellow tongue. It paced behind the glass, moving its head from side to side. It seemed worried.

The front door was about twenty yards away. When I moved towards the door, I bumped into a wall of glass. I turned around to go the other way and bumped into another glass wall. Whichever way I went, my nose hit glass. Glass was all around me, like a huge aquarium. Something was very, very wrong.

Maybe I hit my head when I fell. Did I have a concussion? I raised my hand to feel for a lump. I could see the Komodo's reflection in the glass. It raised one of its front claws and touched its head. I put my hand down and kicked out a foot. The Komodo put down its front claw and stuck out a back one. I moved in closer, and so did the Komodo. We were eye to eye with the wall of glass between us.

Then I looked down at my hands. I couldn't believe what I saw! They were gray and covered with scales, like a Komodo's claws. I twisted to see the rest of my body. I had a tail! A huge, gray, scaly tail! I couldn't believe it. I wasn't looking at the Komodo—I was looking at my own reflection in the glass. I wasn't a boy anymore. Somehow I'd turned into a Komodo dragon!

This couldn't be real. I must have a serious head injury. Maybe I was in the hospital. Or maybe this was a nightmare. That was it. This was just a bad dream. Soon I'd wake up in my own bed. Austin would be in his bed, too. We'd get up and have breakfast. Then we'd go to school. Austin would go to the sixth-grade classroom and I'd go to the eighth-grade. I wouldn't care if he got better grades than I did. I just wanted him to be safe.

I tried to wake up. I closed my eyes and opened them again. All I could see was concrete and a dead rabbit. Glass surrounded me. I squeezed my eyes as tight as I could. I opened them again and looked around. Nothing had changed. I was still a Komodo dragon, and everything around me was strange.

I stretched my legs and tried to move. Slowly, I started forward, scraping my belly on the concrete. Pushing up from my legs, I tried to move again. It was like dragging a mattress. I was much heavier now. My legs—all four of them—were short.

I tried to think. What happened to me? How had I become a Komodo dragon? I'd read about werewolves, people that became wolves when the moon was full. In Greek legends, people who were cursed sometimes turned into animals. Was that what happened to me? Was I dreaming? Was I injured and unconscious? That would be better than being a Komodo dragon.

Worst of all, I worried about Austin. The last time I saw him, he was hanging onto the rail in front of the bear cage. He was screaming and begging me for help. Where was he now? Was he hurt? Was he lying unconscious? Had he blown into a place with dangerous animals? I had to get out of here and find him, fast!

Chapter Two— DART

Out in the parking lot, the teachers were calling for their classes to board the buses. I could hear them as clearly as if they were next to me. One of the teachers asked if anyone had seen Megan Gifford. Someone said she might be with her uncle.

"We're missing Austin Brockway, too," said the teacher. "Has anyone seen him?"

"Luke Brockway isn't on the bus either," said one of the girls. "Maybe Austin is with him."

"We've got to get these kids back to the school." It was the bus driver's voice. "They're cold, wet and scared. Their parents will be waiting."

"What about the missing kids?" asked the teacher. "We can't just leave them here."

I shivered, listening hard. Were they going to leave without us?

"Call zoo security," said the bus driver. "They'll find the lost kids. I'll come back and pick them up after I take this group to the school."

"Where's Roy Gifford?" someone asked. "He's the teacher for bus three."

"Probably looking for his niece, Megan," said the bus driver. "Add his name to the list of those missing and give it to the security guard. We need to get these kids home."

I wanted to get on one of those buses and go home, but I couldn't leave the zoo without Austin. Besides, I was pretty sure the bus driver wasn't going to let a Komodo dragon crawl onto his bus. A bus full of kids was like a box of candy for a Komodo. So I settled down on the cold concrete floor and tried to think. I had to make a plan. How was I going to find my brother? How were we going to get out of here? Most important, how could I change back into a boy?

My stomach growled. I hadn't eaten since breakfast. I was really hungry. Poor Austin. He hadn't even had breakfast. That was my fault. I hit him and gave him a bloody nose. I made him cry. He was so upset, he couldn't eat.

Tears filled my eyes and fell on the cold concrete floor. More than anything, I wanted to find Austin and tell him I was sorry. I wanted to give him his lunch and maybe money for ice cream. I'd lost both our lunch bags during the storm, but I still had money with me. I could buy Austin a hamburger and a shake. Reaching down, I tried to find my pocket. There wasn't one. I didn't even have pants. All I had was a long, scaly body. It was the huge, heavy body of the world's most dangerous lizard.

There must be a way to undo this. First, I had to get out of this glass pen. Then I had to get out of the Reptile House without being seen. Once I was out, I had to find my brother and get him some food. Then I had to find a way to get us both out of here.

Crawling to the corner of the enclosure, I settled down in the pile of hay to think. Komodo dragons could do a lot of things. They could stand on their hind legs. They could run up to twelve miles an hour, maybe faster. They could whip a lot of animals in a fight. They could detect odors a couple of miles away. Maybe I could use Komodo traits to find Austin.

14

I could run fast around the zoo, as long as no one saw me. I could eat anyone who got in my way, but then they'd have to shoot me. Besides, I might look like a Komodo dragon, but inside I was still human. I didn't want to kill anyone. I didn't even want to kill an animal. There had to be another way.

As soon as it was dark, I started to crawl toward the back door of the Komodo enclosure. It was hard to move. I kept trying, pushing up on my four short legs until my body rose above the concrete floor. Snakes bobbed up and down and peered at me from their aquariums. Snakes are nocturnal, active at night. Several pairs of beady snake eyes watched as I shoved myself along. I pushed the dead rabbit out of my way and kept moving. The back door of my enclosure was just ahead. Rising on my hind legs, I crawled up the wall until I was standing. I reached for the latch. It was hard to slide the bolt back with my claws, but I kept trying. Finally the door opened. I was in the back room of the Reptile House, where no visitors were allowed.

I crawled toward the door leading to the outside. It took a long time because my Komodo dragon body was ten feet long, and I wasn't used to having a tail. It smacked against boxes and crates. Above my head was a counter that held the zookeeper's books and papers. Aquariums were back here, too. Turtles, snakes and frogs peered out at me as I waddled past them. Bags of food stood against one wall, but it wasn't food I wanted. The labels read, "Small reptile pellets." I wasn't a small reptile. I was a big, hungry reptile. My brother would be hungry too. I had to find food for both of us. Then I had to find a way to get us home.

Next to the food bags was a big white freezer. At home our freezer was filled with frozen chicken strips, vegetables and ice cream treats. Maybe there was something delicious in this freezer. I lifted the lid and peered in. Bags of frozen rabbits were stacked on one side, bags of frozen rats stacked on the other. In the middle were bags of little gray mice. Frozen mice. Micycles. Yuk.

I pushed myself up to the counter and glanced around. No sandwiches or lunch bags on the counter. I didn't see apples or bananas or anything that looked good to eat. Where could I find people food?

Then I remembered seeing a restaurant at the zoo. There were ice cream carts and hot dog stands, too. I didn't have money now. Even if I did, I couldn't slither into the restaurant and ask for a hamburger. Everyone would scream and run. Getting people food was going to be a problem.

I let myself out the back door and hid behind a long green hedge. Two men were coming down the path. One of them was the zookeeper for the Reptile House. I'd seen him before; his name was Tim. I didn't know the other man, but he wore a zookeeper's uniform, too.

"I've got a sick gecko in the back room," said Tim. "I'll check on him and then meet you in the cafeteria." The other man went down the path away from me. No one else was in sight. It was time to find my brother.

The last time I saw Austin, he was holding onto the rail in front of the grizzly cage. I'd start there. I had to stay out of sight. If anyone saw a Komodo dragon running around loose, they'd call for the DART team. DART stood for Dangerous Animal Response Team. The zoo was filled with dangerous animals. Lions, tigers and bears. Rhinos, crocodiles and venomous snakes. If any of those animals escaped, the DART team would act fast. First they'd try to catch the animal. If they couldn't catch it, they'd shoot it with a powerful drug to make it sleepy. Then they'd put it back where it belonged.

I was a dangerous animal, a Komodo dragon. I couldn't let the DART team capture me. If they found me, they'd shoot me with a tranquilizer gun. Then I'd be asleep, and I couldn't look for Austin.

A delicious aroma wafted through the air. The lady who sold hot dogs was cleaning her stand. Hot dogs and hot dog buns lay scattered everywhere. A string of hot dogs hung from a nearby tree. Hot dogs were under bushes and on the ground next to her cart. They smelled so good my stomach started to growl. When the lady turned her back, I crawled over and gobbled up a few. Then I scurried back to the bushes.

In front of the bear enclosure, zoo workers were raking up trash that had been tossed about by the wind. I waited until they finished. Peeking around the side of the bushes, I checked to be sure no people were there. Then I waddled across the clearing to the grizzly enclosure.

"Austin," I whispered. "Are you here?"

"Luke? Where are you?" The voice came from behind the bars at the front of the enclosure. "I can't see you."

"I'm here. Right next to the bear cage. Where are you?"

"I'm inside the bear cage." His voice sounded sad.

I clambered up the side of the bear cage and looked in. The biggest bear was sitting near the edge, his large furry head resting on the bars. When he heard my voice, the bear's head came up.

"Luke?" He stared down at me. "Is that you?"

I flicked my forked tongue. Standing on my hind legs, I pressed my snout against the metal bars. "Yes, it's me."

The bear stood on his hind legs. "You're a Komodo dragon!"

"You're a grizzly bear."

Austin surveyed his mammoth paws. "That's what I was afraid of. I hoped it was a bad dream."

"It's not a dream. It's a nightmare. Somehow we've become animals. I don't know how it happened."

"Gramps will look for us," said Austin. "Maybe he'll know what happened."

"I hope he knows how to change us back. Meanwhile, we've got to get out of here." I scanned the space behind him. "Where's the door to this cage?"

"I'm afraid to find out. There are two bears back there."

"You're a bear too, dummy. Go look."

Austin lumbered towards the back of the enclosure, staying as far away from the other bears as he could. He nosed around for a few minutes, then stood on his hind legs and patted at the wall. Nothing opened.

"There's no door." His voice was sad. "There's no way out."

I stretched my neck to see better. "There has to be. You got in, didn't you?"

"Yes, but I'm not sure how." Tears welled in his eyes. He looked like a big bad grizzly bear, but inside he was really only a scared little boy. I looked like a Komodo dragon, but I was just a scared kid, too.

The Austin bear sat down with his lower legs stretched out in front of him. He leaned his head against the bars. He hadn't had any breakfast or lunch. He was probably really hungry. Before we tried to escape, I had to find food. I didn't want him weak and fainting. I couldn't carry a seven-hundred pound bear out of here.

"This could take time, Austin. Have you had anything to eat?"

He shook his furry head. "All they gave us was raw fish. I couldn't eat it. You know I hate fish."

This was awful. I had to feed my poor brother, fast.

"I'll find you something to eat, Austin. Wait here."

"Like I'm going anywhere," mumbled Austin.

I crawled away and hid behind the hippo statue. Nearby was an ice-cream cart. No one was manning it. I hurried over and smacked the cart with my tail. The cart fell over on its side. The top came open. All the ice cream goodies fell out onto the pavement. Popsicles, nutty cones and ice cream bars rolled out. Orange pushups tumbled out of their boxes. I swallowed a bunch of ice cream, paper and all. I found a paper bag and pushed cones and pushups into it. Carrying the bag with my teeth, I hurried back to Austin.

Behind me, someone started to scream. "The Komodo is loose! The Komodo is loose!"

Austin clambered up onto his back paws. With a shake of my head, I hurled the ice cream at the bars. Some of the goodies flew into the cage, and some landed on the ledge. Austin stuck out a furry paw and pulled the ice cream towards him.

"Get out of here," he yelled. "Don't let them catch you!"

Zoo employees ran at me from all directions. Two held catch-poles with nooses. A uniformed guard drove up in a golf cart. He was holding a gun, too; one that probably fired real bullets. They wouldn't take any chances. They didn't know I was only an eighth-grade boy. They thought I was a Komodo dragon. If they thought I was going to hurt someone, they'd shoot me. The Komodo would be dead, and so would I. I took off, running as fast as my scaly legs would carry me.

They were fast, but I was faster. Komodos can run twelve miles an hour, and that's more than most humans. I scurried down the main walkway and darted into the African compound. The zoo train waited in the station. The man who drove the train was cleaning the cars. I slid into the driver's seat and pushed the key with my claw. The engine purred. The train rolled forward. The engineer shrieked and dropped his bag of trash. He bellowed, waving his fist in the air.

By the time the DART team arrived on the platform, the train was halfway around the track. I leaped off the train and landed in the field. Zebras, giraffes and kudus scattered. They ran straight into the path of the DART team. I followed the train track through the tunnel and out on the other side. Soon I was back on the main zoo walkway. The DART team was far behind.

Something smelled delicious. Another food stand was closing down. The man who ran it was cleaning the grill. Hamburgers and buns were piled on the counter; boxes of popcorn and bags of cotton candy, too. I hurried to the counter, pulled myself up and gobbled up hamburgers. The man screamed and fled. I shoved several burgers into a bag and clenched it between my teeth. If I hurried, maybe I could throw the bag to Austin before the DART team caught me.

It was too late. Several people in zoo uniforms were running toward me. I turned the corner and headed toward the parking lot. It was a big space with lots of room. I'd let them chase me for a while. Pretty soon they'd get tired. Then I could double back and give my brother some burgers.

"Don't scare him. Let me try to lure him back with food." It was Tim, the zookeeper for the Reptile House.

"Too late! He's heading for the exit," yelled somebody else. "Get the noose over his head. Put him out, now!"

A golf cart pulled up next to me. A rope fell over my head. Something soft was wrapped around my snout so I couldn't open my mouth. I was lifted onto a wagon. I rolled past the grizzlies. A very large bear stood near the edge of the enclosure. I tried to throw him a bag of hamburgers, but it didn't go far. My eyes grew heavier and heavier. Soon I fell asleep.

When I woke up, I was back in the Reptile House. I looked at my reflection in the glass. I was still a Komodo dragon. Austin was still a grizzly bear. He was still hungry, and that was the saddest thing of all.

Chapter Three—Frozen Rats

The next day was Saturday. Austin and I had been in the zoo since Friday morning. People must be missing us by now. What did our teachers think when zoo security didn't find us? Did Gramps call our parents? Did he call the police? It didn't matter. The police could look for us day and night, but they wouldn't find us. Not while we were trapped in the bodies of animals.

My escape attempt had failed. I hadn't rescued Austin, either. But at least he knew he wasn't kept here alone. He knew I was here, and that I'd help him.

Austin was in danger. I was alone in my cage, but he was with two other bears. What if they tried to hurt him? He wouldn't know how to protect himself. Austin got good grades at school, but didn't know much about animals. It was up to me. He was my brother. I had to help him survive until we got out of here.

Tim opened the back door of the Komodo enclosure and stepped inside. The veterinarian was with him. They stayed by the door, watching me.

"How are you, old buddy?" Tim slid a rabbit across the concrete floor toward me.

I sniffed the rabbit. He must have nuked it in the microwave, because it was warm. It smelled disgusting. No way was I going to eat that thing. I crawled away and flopped down in the straw.

What was Austin having for dinner? Bears ate fish and berries. He hated fish. I hoped they gave him some berries. I wished they'd give me something else, too. I was hungry enough to eat vegetables. Cabbage, even. Anything but raw rabbit.

"He's off his food," said the veterinarian. He squatted down to stare at me, and I read his nametag. Bob Hartley, DVM, Doctor of Veterinary Medicine.

"He didn't eat last night, either," said Tim. "He usually likes rabbits."

Doctor Hartley had a syringe with a long needle in his hand. Was he going to give me a shot?

"Hold him steady while I take a blood sample," said Dr. Hartley.

I didn't like the sound of that. I'd had shots before, but never with a needle that long.

"This won't hurt a bit, old buddy," said Tim. The vet took blood from my tail. I didn't even feel it.

"This Komodo has red scales on the top of his head," said the vet.

Tim frowned. "No, he doesn't. He's all gray."

"Look." The vet gently touched my head.

Tim bent over to have a closer look. "You're right. He never had those red scales before. Maybe he got injured when we moved him onto the wagon."

I studied my reflection in the glass. I couldn't see the top of my head. All I could see was my ugly Komodo face and my scaly gray legs with claws.

Another man was staring at me through the outside window of the Komodo pen. It was Gramps! I was so glad to see him I almost yelled. Luckily, I closed my mouth just in time. If Tim and the vet heard me talking, they'd probably put me in an animal hospital and do experiments on me. Then I'd never get out.

Tim was still watching me. I put my head down and tried not to appear too excited. After a few minutes, Tim and the vet left. The front door of the Reptile House opened and Gramps entered the room.

I crawled up and pushed my snout against the glass. Gramps bent down and put his hand against the window.

He whispered, "Luke, is that you?"

"It's me, Gramps!"

"I figured you were here." Gramps rubbed his neck. He looked very tired. He'd probably been up all night waiting for zoo security to find us.

Before they left, Mom and Dad told us not to upset Gramps. They said he was old and couldn't handle the stress. I hoped he wouldn't have a heart attack from seeing his grandsons turned into zoo creatures.

"Gramps, did you see Austin? Is he all right? Did they feed him?"

"He's in the bear cage, eating berries. What did they give you?"

"Frozen rats. Today they gave me a rabbit. The fur is still on it."

"Yuk." Gramps made a face. "I'll bet you'll never complain about my cooking again."

"I'll never complain about anything again."

I swished my tail back and forth on the concrete floor. I was glad Tim was gone, because I needed to talk to Gramps. I had a lot of questions.

"What happened to us, Gramps?"

He shook his head and sighed. "It's a long story. I'd better get a chair."

He found a metal one nearby and pulled it close to the Komodo enclosure. He looked around to make sure no one else could hear us. Bending his head down to the glass, he whispered, "You were cursed, Luke."

I flicked my forked tongue at him. "Cursed? What do you mean?"

23

Gramps scratched his head. He started to speak, and then stopped. He seemed to be having trouble finding the right words. After a minute, he went on.

"This curse has been in our family for years. No one has been changed in a long time, and I thought it had died out. Somehow you two activated it again."

I shook my head and flicked my forked tongue. "What curse? You never said anything about that."

"I don't like to talk about it. I don't want people to think I'm crazy."

"You're sitting on a chair talking to a Komodo dragon. If anybody sees you, they'll definitely think you're crazy."

Gramps rested his elbows on his knees and stared at the floor. His face was sad.

I tapped my thick nails on the glass. "So what about this curse? Is it like turning into a werewolf or something?"

He sat up and peered at me over his half-glasses. "When the conditions are right, metamorphoses like this can take place at the sub-atomic level."

"Speak English, Gramps. I don't understand."

He gestured with his arm back and forth across the room. "Everything is made of energy—people, animals, trees, even rocks. We are all part of one big energy field." He made a circling motion with his hand. "The energy vibrates at various rates of speed. Thought energy vibrates very fast and transforms easily. The energy in living things vibrates pretty fast too. The energy in rocks is much slower, so you can't see them change."

I paced back and forth inside the glass enclosure, watching him. "I still don't get it. How did we become animals?"

Gramps tried again to explain, speaking more slowly. "Remember when you two were fighting yesterday morning?"

I blinked. Was that only yesterday? It seemed like ages ago.

24

Gramps went on. "Austin said he'd rather have a Komodo dragon for a brother. You said you'd rather have a grizzly bear. Remember that? You wished each other to be different."

I nodded. We'd yelled that at each other in the car on the way to school.

Gramps pointed to the sky. "The electromagnetic field is all around us. When the lightning struck, it altered the electromagnetic field. That caused the energy waves to scramble. The energy from your thoughts created what you both wanted." He sat back, shaking his head. "That's what the curse does. During a certain kind of storm, you get what you wish."

It seemed too weird to be true. "I wished for a pepperoni pizza, too, Gramps. Why didn't I get that wish?"

Gramps shrugged. "You and Austin were really angry. Anger carries a lot of energy. It's partly my fault, too. I said you were both acting like you belonged in a zoo. So I added the force of my energy to yours."

He bent down, looking at me closely. "Did you know you have red scales on top of your head? I wonder if that's because you have red hair. When you're a human, I mean."

I flicked my forked tongue at him. "I don't care about the red scales. What can we do now? How do we get out of this?"

"We have to wait until the conditions are right again."

"You mean we can't change back until there's another storm? We could be here for weeks!"

"The weather is going to be bad again in a couple of days. We might be able to attract lightning to strike the water tower and alter the electromagnetic field again."

"Is that all?"

"Not quite. You and Austin have to do your part, too. You have to be thinking the right thoughts when lightning strikes. Otherwise it might not work."

"You mean we might not become boys again?" My words came out in a terrified shriek.

25

Gramps shook his head. "Calm down. That's not what I said."

He took a deep breath. "You have to wish to be your old self again. To be human. You have to want your brother to be his old self, just the way he was. He has to wish the same about you. You both have to give the thought all your energy."

"We can do that. I know we can. Just be sure to tell Austin." I flopped down in the straw. I was tired of pacing around my glass enclosure.

"I have to do my part, too," said Gramps. "I have to say you belong at home, with me. That won't be hard, because that *is* what I think."

"I want Austin to be home and safe, Gramps. I want that more than anything."

Gramps smiled. "Good."

I would do anything to get Austin back home, even if it meant I had to stay here. More than anything, I wanted my brother to be safe.

I took a deep breath. "So now all we have to do is wait for lightning to strike, right?"

Gramps rubbed his chin. "There are a few other requirements, but we'll talk about those later. First, I have to figure out how to attract lightning to the zoo without anyone getting hurt."

"What about a lightning rod?"

"We'd have to position it at the top of the water tower to make the lightning hit. It has to be a strong enough strike to alter the electromagnetic field."

He thought for a minute. "I can get a lightning rod, but somebody will have to take it up there. I can't do it. It's a long way up, and I'm too old."

"I can't do it either. I'm afraid of heights."

"I know. Don't worry, we'll find someone."

What if we didn't? I was being a coward. If it was the only way to save my brother, I'd do it. I'd take the lightning rod up to

26

the top of the water tower. The only problem was I was a Komodo dragon now. Komodos could climb partway up a tree to catch prey, but I didn't think they could climb water towers. What we needed was a monkey.

Gramps stayed at the zoo all day, going back and forth between the Reptile House and the Grizzly Bear exhibit. At noon he went to the café for a hot dog and a cup of coffee. Then he came back to visit me again. He had a bag of food from the café. Glancing around, he made sure no one was within hearing range.

"I tried to get these hot dogs to Austin," said Gramps. "But there were too many people around. I couldn't take the chance. I'll try again when I leave you."

At four o'clock, the security guard came into the Reptile House.

"The zoo is closing in fifteen minutes, sir. Please start making your way back to the gate." The security guard held the door open, waiting for Gramps to exit.

Gramps bent his head down to the cage. "Don't worry, Luke. We'll figure this out. Eat your rabbit. You have to stay strong."

"Gramps, if you can't get that food to Austin, hide it in the bushes. I'll try to bring it to him later, when it's dark."

"Be careful, Luke. Don't let them catch you. I'll see you tomorrow." With that, he left.

I nosed the rabbit. It looked like a stuffed animal I used to keep on my bed. It had the same kind of nose and puffy little tail. But this one smelled bad. There was no way I could eat it. I pushed it under some straw so I wouldn't have to see it. I'd try to sneak out again later and find some real food. This time I'd have to be extra careful. If I got caught again, they'd probably put a padlock on my door.

A few minutes later, Tim came to check my water supply. He stood at the back of my enclosure and peered in at me.

"How're you doing, buddy?" He looked toward the pile of straw in the corner. The rabbit's back paws were sticking out from under the straw. It looked like the rabbit was trying to hide from me.

"You didn't eat your rabbit," said Tim. "How about some mice? Want some nice mice?"

I didn't want any nice mice. I closed my eyes and ignored him. I wanted him to go away so I could think. Tim didn't go away. He came closer and bent down, squinting at the top of my head.

"You must have been hurt out there yesterday. You're not acting like yourself at all."

I lifted my head and flicked my tongue. I wanted to tell Tim to bring me a double cheeseburger and some fries. I didn't try to say it. I didn't want him to faint at hearing a talking Komodo. So I put my head down again and closed my eyes. Soon Tim went away.

Outside, the sun was going down. I waited until it was completely dark, and then quietly slid out of my glass cage. There was a new lock on the back door of the Reptile House. The lock had a deadbolt. It was the same kind of sliding bolt we had on our doors at home. That lock might keep ordinary Komodos in, but not a kid who knew how to open it. I pulled myself up against the wall. Then I slid the bolt back with my right claw. Lowering myself to the floor, I crawled out into the cool night air.

Where was that bag of food Gramps brought? I checked the bushes, but couldn't find it. I looked behind the Reptile House. No bag there, either.

The lights were still on in the restaurant kitchen. A cook came out and dumped leftovers into the trash can. I waited behind a hedge until she turned out the kitchen lights. After a few minutes she left the building. She headed down the path toward the employee parking lot.

I flicked my forked tongue to taste the air. I detected no humans, so I hurried over to the trash cans. I tipped them over one at a time and sorted through the trash with my claws. I gobbled up hot dogs, ketchup and chunks of cheeseburger. In the last trash can, I found a lot of food. There was a half-empty carton of milk, a half-eaten chicken sandwich and rinds of watermelon. I pushed all of this and several half-eaten hot dogs into a paper bag. Carrying the bag between my teeth, I crept toward the bear enclosure. I stayed close to the cages and away from the lights. When I reached the bear cage, I pushed myself up and looked in.

"Austin." I kept my voice low. "Are you awake?"

A bear meandered to the side of the cage. "Luke, is that you?"

"Do you know any other talking Komodos?" I flung the bag onto the concrete ledge at the front of his enclosure. Austin reached his paw through the bars to grab it. He tore it open and stuffed his mouth with food.

"Thanks, Luke. They gave me raw fish today. I couldn't eat it. If there's anything I hate worse than tuna salad, it's raw fish."

Two other bears were sleeping near the back of the enclosure. I raised my claw and pointed at them. "Are those other bears bothering you?"

"Not yet. I stay on my side of the cage and they stay on theirs. The floor is hard and it stinks in here. Those bears pee and poop anywhere they want. They act like animals."

"They are animals, Austin."

The Austin bear snorted. "Oh, yeah. Anyway, it's disgusting."

He pulled a half-eaten hot dog from the bag and popped it into his mouth. He stuck his nose in the bag and rooted around for a few minutes, making chewing noises. Then he held the bag upside-down and shook it. A couple of bits of bread fell out. He picked them up carefully and popped them in his mouth. It was sad to see my brother so hungry. That little bag didn't hold enough food to feed that big bear body. He put his massive head on the bars and growled. The sound was long and low, like a moan.

"Don't worry." I put my snout up close to the bars and lowered my voice. "Gramps and I are working on a plan to turn us back into humans. As soon as we figure it out, Gramps will come and tell you how. Now I have to get back to the Reptile House before the night guard makes his rounds."

He waved his paw. I scurried back to the Reptile House and flopped down in the corner of my cage. When the night guard appeared, he shined a light in my eyes. I hadn't seen this man before. He was about Gramps height, but thinner. He walked with a limp, as though his leg hurt him. He didn't smile. I flicked my tongue at him a couple of times.

He narrowed his eyes and scowled at me. "You think you're pretty tough, don't you. I've seen animals a lot tougher than you, old boy. When I tell you to back away, you do it or you'll get a taste of this." He banged the glass with a short metal rod. I'd never seen anything like it. I flicked my tongue and tasted the air, but I couldn't tell what it was.

Then the guard went around the back and came into my space. He walked right up to me, closer than Tim usually did. Didn't this man know anything? Komodos eat humans. I flicked my forked tongue at him, warning him to back away.

The guard didn't look worried. He leaned down, grinning at me with yellow teeth. It was a stupid thing for him to do. I wanted to take a chunk out of him right then and there, just to show him how stupid it was.

Suddenly he jabbed the end of the metal thing into my underbelly. A sharp, stinging pain stabbed through me. I screamed and jumped! It hurt a lot, like getting bitten by a hundred wasps all at the same time. My legs went stiff, and then I fell flat on my belly.

The night guard grinned again, showing all his yellow teeth. His cheeks bunched up, making his eyes into little slits. He held up the metal rod. "That's to show you who's boss around here. When I tell you to back up, you better do it."

I closed my eyes. The place where he jabbed me burned like it was on fire. I stayed as still as I could, trying to play dead. He poked my side with his foot. I wanted to bite his leg off, but I didn't. If I bit him, I'd be put to sleep for good. After a few minutes, he left.

I straightened my short lizard legs and limped to my water pan. My belly was still burning. I wanted to put water on it, but there wasn't enough in the pan. I needed ice. I made my way out of the glass enclosure and into the back room. Lifting the door of the freezer, I sorted through the bags and found a nice big rabbit, frozen stiff. I carried it back to my pen and stretched my belly across it. I'd never eat the rabbit, but it made a good ice pack.

As I lay there, I tried to decide what to do next. The night guard was mean. How many other animals had he stung with that metal rod? I was sure the zookeepers didn't know about this practice. If they did, they'd tell the zoo manager, and the manager would fire that guard. If only I could tell Tim. Tim cared about us. He'd get that guard fired for sure.

Then I remembered Gramps would come to visit me in the morning. I could tell Gramps what the security guard did to me. Gramps would know what to do.

Chapter Four—The Death Adder

The next morning, a new snake arrived at the Reptile House. The snake exhibits were across from my enclosure, so I could watch all the activity. Tim and the vet opened a box and let the snake crawl into its new home.

The vet bent down and peered into the glass rectangle. "Where did it go?"

"Under those leaves," said Tim. "See that bit of red?"

The volunteer came in to view the new arrival. She stepped closer and looked into the aquarium. "It's so small. Is it a juvenile?"

Tim shook his head. "It's only twelve inches long, but it's fully grown. They don't usually get longer than about thirty inches."

The volunteer squinted at the glass box, frowning. "What kind of snake is it?"

"A Death Adder."

"That sounds scary," said the volunteer.

"It is scary," said Tim. "The Death Adder has one of the quickest strikes of any snake in the world. Its venom is deadly."

The volunteer opened her notebook. "We learned about this snake in our training last week. It can strike several times before the victim even knows what hit him. The venom paralyzes the prey." She shivered. "What a dangerous snake."

Tim came in through the back door of my cage. He filled my water dish and swept up the dirty straw. I got up and tried to move. I still didn't feel too well.

Tim poked the rabbit I'd used as an ice pack. "You didn't eat your rabbit. You usually like rabbits. Maybe I'd better have the vet take a look at you again."

If there was only some way to tell him what happened. I stared at him, trying to look pained.

"What's the matter?" Tim frowned at me. "You look like you're trying to tell me something."

I wanted to tell him something, all right. I wanted to tell him how the night guard burned me with that metal rod he carried. But I just put my head down and closed my eyes. Pretty soon Tim left my enclosure.

Gramps came as soon as the zoo opened for visitors. I was glad to see him.

"We'll have to talk quickly," said Gramps. "People will come to see the new snake."

He pulled up his chair and bent forward. I rolled over and Gramps saw the red mark on my belly. I told him what happened.

"I can't believe it!" Gramps was so angry he was yelling. "Imagine! Bullying a helpless animal!"

"Gramps, lower your voice. Someone will hear you."

"That night guard abused you! I won't stand for it!" Gramps paced back and forth in front of my glass pen. I paced back and forth next to him on the other side of the glass.

"He's a dangerous bully. We have to stop him." He made a fist and slammed it into his other hand.

I wanted to stop the guard, too, but I wanted to get us out of this place first. I edged up close to the glass again. "Did you think of a way to get us out?"

"The weather is supposed to get stormy around ten tomorrow night. There will be a lot of thunder and lightning. If I can get the lightning to strike near the zoo, there's a good chance you can become human again. So you and Austin have to be ready."

That was great news. I'd be ready, and I'd make sure Austin was, too.

"What do we do, Gramps?"

"Stand as close as you can to the edge of the cage. Think the right thoughts. Wish as hard as you can to be your old self."

"No problem there. I'm wishing that all the time."

"But you have to be holding the thought in your mind when the lightning strikes." Gramps pointed at me. "You can't let yourself be distracted. Even if an elephant comes and dances in front of you, you have to stay focused. Understand?"

"That's all there is to it?" I couldn't believe it. It couldn't be that simple.

Gramps scratched his chin. "I haven't told you everything. It's possible something could go wrong."

I flicked my forked tongue at him. "Like what?"

"This doesn't happen every day," said Gramps, "so I don't know for sure." He held up his hand, counting on his fingers. "First, when you change back to humans, the old animals will come back. They could land inside or outside their cages. You could land inside or outside the cages. You could be outside the cage with the animal, or inside the cage with the animal."

We could wind up inside the cage together? That wouldn't be good. I might get out, but Austin would be in with three grizzlies.

Gramps held up another finger. "Here's another thing that could go wrong. If the power goes off, the security fences will go down. A lot of animals could get out of their enclosures, including the dangerous ones. We have to be ready for anything."

I didn't care if all the animals got out and stood on their heads. I just wanted to go home.

I rolled over onto my side, trying to take the weight off my burned belly. "But the lightning will strike, right?"

Gramps nodded. "Probably, but you must be prepared for anything. If you end up in the cage with the Komodo, walk calmly to the back and let yourself out."

I nodded. I knew how to get out. I'd been doing that for two days. Austin was the one who could be in danger.

"Gramps, what about Austin? What if he's inside with the bears? One human doesn't stand a chance against a grizzly, let alone three."

Gramps sighed. "That's a bigger problem."

"He'll need a way to keep the bears at a distance until we can get him out," I said. "He needs a weapon."

"Weapon?" Gramps took a deep breath. "Like what?"

"What about that cattle prod the night guard carries?"

"We'll have to get it away from the guard," said Gramps. "I'll figure out a way to do that."

Then I had another idea. "What if we gave the other bears tranquilizers and put them to sleep?"

Gramps slapped his knee. "That's a good idea, Luke!"

"They have tranquilizer guns here. I'm sure the vet has one, maybe in this building."

"If only we knew somebody on the staff," said Gramps.

I shook my head. "I see Tim every day, but I can't just start talking to him. He'll think he's gone crazy."

Gramps stood up. "There's one other problem I haven't told you about."

I flicked my forked tongue. "Like what?"

Gramps sighed. "You and Austin aren't the only humans that got trapped in animal bodies during the storm."

Gramps told me that two other people, a man and a little girl, never returned from the school trip to the zoo. The man's name was Roy Gifford. He was the gym teacher at my school. His niece, Megan, was also missing. Now we had a new problem to worry about. We couldn't leave them here as animals.

"They're both in the zoo somewhere," said Gramps. "Keep your eyes and ears open. We have to find them. We'll have to help them escape, too."

"Why are they here? Is there a curse on their family, too?"

Gramps shrugged. "I don't know. I've never heard of this happening in any family but ours."

Then a lot of visitors came into the Reptile House. They gathered around the new snake exhibit. The volunteer started to tell them about the Death Adder.

Gramps looked at his watch. "I'm going to the café for lunch. Then I'll go see Austin. I'll come back to visit you again later."

A little boy pointed at Gramps. "Mommy, that man is talking to the big lizard." The woman turned to look. Gramps quickly left the building.

It was a long day. Gramps went back and forth between Austin and me. We couldn't talk again, because the building was crowded with people. I was still glad to see him, though. Austin and I weren't alone. Gramps would help us get out of here.

A security guard came into the Reptile House. I recognized him. It was the man who struck me with that metal rod in my belly and burned me.

"Gramps," I whispered. "That's him. That's the guard who hurt me."

The guard limped over to where Gramps was standing. He pointed to his wristwatch. "It's four o'clock, sir. The zoo is closing. It's time for all visitors to leave."

Gramps glared at him. "This Komodo has a burn mark on his belly. That's not a good way to take care of these animals."

"A burn mark? I don't think so," said the guard. "There's nothing hot in there."

"It looks like somebody burned him," said Gramps. "You're the security guard, right? You're supposed to protect these animals. I'll be talking to the director of the zoo about this."

The guard put his hands on his hips and stared at Gramps. He was about the same height as Gramps but the looked a lot meaner. "Talk to anybody you want, mister. But you'll have to do it tomorrow. The zoo is closed and you have to leave."

Gramps put his face close to the guard's. "I've seen you somewhere before. What's your name?" He squinted at the guard's nametag. "Dunn Nikowski. Is that right?"

"That's right. The zoo opens again at ten tomorrow morning. You can come back then."

Gramps looked down at me, and then back at the guard. "I'll be talking to the zookeeper about that burn. I'd better not find any other marks on him tomorrow or I'll hold you personally responsible. You got that, Mr. Nikowski?" He poked the guard in the chest.

"Sure," said the guard. He grinned. He had a gold tooth like a pirate. "Don't worry about this old fellow. He'll be fine."

After Gramps left, Dunn bent down and narrowed his eyes at me. "That old man doesn't scare me. If I have any trouble with you, I'll fix you good. Got that?"

Just then the door to my enclosure opened. Tim came in. He was carrying something furry. Dunn waved to him and went out the front door. I was glad to see him go. With Dunn gone, I was safe, at least for a little while.

Tim slid another rabbit across the floor. It stopped in front of me. I felt like puking, but I just put my head down on the floor and closed my eyes. Tim took out his cell phone and made a call.

A few minutes later, the vet arrived. "Is the Komodo sick?"

"I don't know," said Tim. "He's still off his food. He seems depressed."

They squatted down next to me. I rolled onto my side so they could see my belly.

Tim pointed. "Look at that mark! He's been wounded."

The vet scratched his head. "It looks like a burn."

"How would he get a burn?" asked Tim. He sounded worried. "There's nothing hot in here. It's not like he's out wandering the zoo when we're not here."

I bit down hard to keep from laughing.

"I've seen marks like that on other animals," said the vet. "I don't understand it. I wasn't on duty when he got out. Did the DART team use anything on him? A stun gun, maybe?"

"He was heading for the parking lot and we couldn't catch him. You know how fast they are. So they shot him with a tranquilizer gun. He struggled in the net before they got him up off the ground. Maybe that's when it happened."

"I don't think so. It doesn't look like a scrape. Wait a minute." The vet scratched his chin. "I just thought of something."

"What?"

"When I was in veterinary school, they used a cattle prod on a bull that escaped. He had a mark just like that on his rump."

"Who would have a cattle prod?" asked Tim.

"Anybody who works with large animals might have one. We used to keep one here, in the cupboard."

"We'd better see if it's still there." Tim pushed at the rabbit with his boot. "He's not eating rabbits or the rats. That's not like him. Usually he gobbles them right up."

"Try chicken," said the vet. "Or maybe ground hamburger and rice. Something bland." They walked out, still chatting.

I could hear them in the back room. I hoped they'd leave soon. It was getting dark. I needed to get to those trash cans before they were emptied.

Tim came out of the back room with food for the crocodile. He stayed behind the safety door and tossed in what looked like a big chunk of beef. The croc was a big fellow, almost seventeen feet long. He was one of the most dangerous creatures in the zoo. What if he got out when we changed back into humans? Gramps said we could wind up inside the enclosures with the animals. I wouldn't want to land anywhere near that crocodile.

I waddled to the edge of my enclosure and peered through the glass at the snakes. Snakes are nocturnal, so they're more active at night. Their heads were bobbing as though they were looking around. I didn't have time to watch them, though. I had to find the gym teacher and his niece. They were here in the zoo somewhere. Gramps said the thunderstorms would probably arrive tomorrow, so I'd have to find them tonight. The zoo was huge. There were at least three thousand species. How could I locate these two? I needed help. I needed someone smart, someone who knew how to plan. I needed Austin.

Austin was very intelligent. He knew how to think and plan. His science project won first place at the state science fair. When Tim and the vet left, I'd go outside, pull out real food from the trash can and take it to Austin. Then we'd figure out how to find Mr. Gifford and his niece.

I heard something strange. It sounded like crying. No, it was softer than crying. It was more like a kitten mewing. It was a tiny, squeaky sound.

"Help me! Help me, someone! I'm trapped!" The voice was coming from one of the snake exhibits.

I stretched my neck and peered through the glass. "Who's out there?"

"Me. I'm over here," said the small voice.

Someone was trapped here in the reptile house, in a reptile's body. It had to be small, from the sound. A very tiny reptile. A small snake, maybe. Maybe it was the gym teacher or his niece.

I called out as loud as I could, "I can't see you. Where are you?"

"I'm on the highest part of this exhibit. Can you see me?"

I squinted. It was hard to see anything in the dim light. "I can't see you. Tell me what's around you."

"I'm up on a log. The log has bumps that look like warts."

I knew which exhibit had that sort of log. I'd seen it when I first came to look at the Komodo. It was the corner pen in the row across from my enclosure.

I called out again, "What color are you?"

"Red," said the little voice. "I'm small. Only about a foot long, I think."

Red. Twelve inches long. This was bad. This was worse than bad. The little voice was coming from the Death Adder. The Death Adder had a lightning-fast strike and poisonous venom. It could kill anyone who tried to rescue it. Kill them fast.

As I stared at the Death Adder's aquarium, a small red snake crawled out from under some leaves.

"I see you. Can you see me? I'm the Komodo dragon."

There was a little squeak, as if the little snake was in pain. "So it's true. We're animals. I was hoping this was a nightmare and I'd wake up." The snake squealed again. "I want to go home."

I called out, "I can't talk to you when you're crying. Let me know when you're finished."

There were a couple more sniffs, and then it was quiet again.

"That's better." I tried to sound cheerful, even though I didn't feel that way. "What's your name?"

"Megan. Megan Gifford."

"We're not going to stay this way, Megan. My grandfather is working on a plan to change us back. I'm glad we found you, so you can transform back, too. Now we just have to locate your uncle."

The snake sniffed. "The last time I saw him, he was going into the Primate Forest. He likes the great apes."

"Thanks. I'll look there."

"Your voice sounds familiar," said the snake. "What's your name?"

"Luke Brockway. My brother Austin is here, too."

She squealed again. "I know Austin. He's in my advanced math class."

I let out a long breath. "My brother is advanced at everything."

"I'm sure you're good at a lot of things, too," said the snake.

I couldn't think of a single thing I was good at, so I didn't answer.

The red snake's head bobbed back and forth above the log. "You said you'd look for my uncle tonight. How can you do that? Aren't you trapped there?"

"There's a door in my exhibit that leads to the back room. The back room has a door to the outside. I have to leave now, Megan. I have to find food."

"Can I go with you? I don't want to stay here with all these scary snakes around me."

"You're the scariest snake in here. Besides, I can't take you with me. It's too dangerous. If they see the Komodo is outside its glass, they'll try to capture me. They'd capture you, too. Anything could happen." She could kill me by accident. I decided not to mention that.

The red snake's head went still. "I understand. What will you do?"

"I'll hide behind bushes. When there's no one around, I'll try to get something to eat."

"Could you get something for me, too? I'd love a piece of fruit."

Did she think this was a take-out restaurant? She probably didn't know I had to carry bags of food with my teeth.

"I'm sorry to be a bother," said the Megan snake. "But I haven't had anything to eat since that terrible storm. They gave me some awful-smelling worm paste, but I couldn't eat it. What do they feed you?"

"Frozen rats and nice mice."

"Yuk." She made a gagging sound.

42

A few minutes later I crawled out the back door. The air felt funny. The scales along my spine began to prickle. Something was going to happen, any minute.

Thunder rumbled in the distance. Did Gramps have his timing right? If the storm arrived tonight, what would we do? We weren't ready. If we weren't ready when the storm hit, we would be animals for the rest of our lives.

Chapter Five—Revenge is Sweet

Bolts of lightning shot across the dark sky. That worried me. Gramps said the storm wouldn't get bad until tomorrow. I hoped he was right, because we weren't prepared. There was a lot to think about.

Bad things could happen. I could end up inside the glass enclosure with the real Komodo dragon. Austin could be in a cage with three grizzly bears. The lightning could knock the power out. The power to the electric safety fences would go off. Animals might get out and walk free inside the zoo. They might even escape the zoo and go into the neighborhood. What would happen if the lions got out? Or the rhinoceroses? Or the tigers? No one would be safe. Anyone who went outside their house could be attacked. Calling the police wouldn't help. They couldn't arrest a rhinoceros even if they could catch it. The fire department couldn't help either. Elephants like water. An elephant could pick up a water hose with its trunk and turn it on the firemen. Angry elephants would trample fences and eat the gardens. Giraffes would eat the trees. Lions, tigers, the Komodo and the crocodile would eat people. We needed a way to defend ourselves. We had to make a plan.

First, I had to find Mr. Gifford, the gym teacher. Megan said he'd gone to see the great apes before the storm started. If he was near the Primate Forest, he could be a monkey now. He could be a chimpanzee, or even a gorilla. Whatever he was, if I didn't get to him before the next storm, he wouldn't know what happened to him, or how to change form again. He couldn't teach gym if he was covered with fur and swinging from the flagpole.

I was worried about Megan, too. If she ended up as a human in the snake aquarium with the real Death Adder, she'd be dead in seconds. We had to get her out of there and take her with us. She could bite one of us accidentally. So much could go wrong. It would be a miracle if we became our real selves and made it home alive.

The rain started. The drops fell gently at first. The cold rain felt good. I rolled over in the dirt and let the rain fall on my sore belly. The cold water took the sting out of the burn.

"Let's get inside," said a man.

I recognized his voice. It was Dunn Nikowski, the guard with the cattle prod. There was another security guard with him. Dunn had a strange gait. He moved as though his right leg didn't work correctly. I slid behind a long hedge and kept quiet. He and his buddy walked right past me. I held my breath. The second guard took a bottle out of his pocket and drank from it. He offered the bottle to Dunn, but Dunn refused. I didn't know what was in that bottle, but I didn't think it was lemonade.

Dunn's voice was low. "These animals do exactly what I tell them to do. They all know better than to mess with me." They kept walking, and I didn't hear anything else.

When they were out of sight, I waddled to the trash cans behind the restaurant. The lights were out in the kitchen. That meant the kitchen staff had gone home and it was safe to search for food.

I tipped one of the cans over and began to nose through the scraps. I could smell meat. Like yesterday, there were leftover hamburger and hot dogs and some messy stuff that smelled like barbequed beef. I found a bag and shoved in hot dogs, buns, ice cream cones and French fries. Megan wanted fruit, but I didn't see any. The next trash can held pieces of chicken, cookies and a whole cheese sandwich. I shoved those into a bag, too. Austin was a big bear, and he needed a lot to eat. Holding the bags with my teeth, I crawled toward the bear cage.

Austin was waiting for me. His huge head rested against the bars. There was no one around, so I pushed myself up on my hind legs.

"Hey, Austin," I said in a loud whisper. "Here's some food." I pitched the bag to the ledge where Austin could reach it. He slid his paw through the bars and grabbed the bag. He pushed his nose down into it and began to chomp. A few scraps fell on the floor and he gobbled them up in one slurp. He even licked the ketchup from the inside of the bag.

"Thanks, Luke." His voice sounded funny. When he put his head against the bars again, I knew something was wrong. His stomach rumbled. He wasn't eating the raw fish they gave him, and I couldn't find enough hot dogs to fill up such a large bear.

I hated that my brother was hungry. We'd never been hungry before, in our whole lives—at least not for long. When we came home from school, Mom gave us a snack. If we were hungry after a game, Dad bought us ice cream. Gramps prepared a good breakfast and a good dinner. He packed lots of goodies in our lunch bags. Our family took care of us and made sure we had enough to eat. Now, because of some stupid curse, we had become starving animals.

I crawled under the chains in front of the bear cage and climbed to the ledge so I could talk to him. "We're breaking out of here tomorrow, Austin. You need more food so you can stay strong. I'll check the trash cans behind the hot dog stand."

Austin shook his furry head. "They've picked those up already. Besides, the hunger isn't so bad. It's my right paw." He held it out. There was a long mark where it looked like the fur had been scraped off. "It hurts a lot."

"How did that happen?" I peered at the wound. It looked like a burn.

"The night guard hit me with something," said Austin. "It had prongs on the end. It gave me a terrible shock. The guard told me to back away from the bars, but I couldn't move fast enough. So he stuck that rod on my paw and zinged me. It really hurt." He pulled his paw away from me. "He'll be coming around again tonight. This time I'll stay out of his way."

Anger roiled up in me. I was so angry I wanted to punch that night guard right in the teeth and wipe away his evil grin.

"I know who you mean. He got me, too, right across my stomach." I showed Austin the mark on my belly.

Now Austin was angry. "How could he do that to you? You're just a helpless animal."

"So are you." I flicked my forked tongue a couple of times. "Actually, we're not that helpless. Either one of us could eat him in about five seconds."

The corners of his mouth turned up. "Too bad he's too dumb to know that." Austin put his head on the bars again. "What about tomorrow?"

I crouched on the ground next to him and told him about Gramps' plan. "He's been watching the weather. It will take place tomorrow night. We have to be ready. Did you find that door yet?"

He pointed toward the back of his space. "In there. See that big stone? There's a door behind it." Austin put his head down against the bars again. "What if it doesn't work, Luke? What if we're trapped here forever?"

"We won't be," I stated firmly. "We're getting out of here tomorrow. We just have to be prepared in case anything goes wrong."

Austin narrowed his beady little bear eyes. "What do you mean?"

I tasted the air with my tongue. There were humans around, and they were close. I had to talk quickly. "When the lightning strikes, we have to be thinking the right thoughts. You have to wish you were human again. You have to wish I was human again, too. You have to be thinking those things when the lightning strikes. It's the only way to undo the curse."

Austin gripped the bars of the cage with his paws and stared at me. "What if I forget? All I can think about is food. I don't want to turn into a pizza."

"That's why you have to focus." The people were getting closer. I talked faster. "There's one other problem. Gramps doesn't know where we'll be when we change back. It's possible you could end up in this cage with the bears again...only this time you'll be a boy. I'll find you a weapon so you can protect yourself."

Suddenly Austin dropped down onto all fours. "Get down. Someone's coming."

I scurried under the nearby bushes. The voices grew louder. In a few seconds, Dunn Nikowski and another night guard approached the grizzly bear exhibit. Dunn ducked under the chains that separated the visitor path from the bear enclosure. He came right up to the front of the cage.

"All the animals here respect me." Dunn tapped his chest. He was showing off for his buddy. "They do exactly what I tell them. Even if they are big and dangerous, they do what I say. Watch this." He took the cattle prod out from under his jacket.

The other guard grabbed Dunn's hand. "Don't use that. If the zookeepers find out, you'll be fired."

"Who's going to tell them? You?" Dunn glared at the other man.

"Not me. My mouth stays shut."

49

Dunn poked him in the chest. "If you say one word about this, I'll tell them about that bottle you keep in your pocket."

Laughing, Dunn moved closer to the bear cage. "Remember me? You're supposed to back up out of the way when I show up." Austin had backed away, but not far enough.

"You'll remember after this." Dunn reached in with the cattle prod and struck Austin's back leg. Austin's huge furry body went stiff. He screamed with pain as the electricity shot through him.

In that second, I forgot I was a Komodo. I jumped out from behind the hedge and ran at Dunn as fast as I could, baring all my teeth. I wanted to kill him for hurting my brother. I pounced on him and knocked him to the ground.

The other guard screamed and took off running. I was faster. I caught him easily and knocked him down with my tail. A brown bottle fell out of his jacket. I plucked it up with my teeth and headed back to where Dunn lay. He had the cattle prod in one hand and his cell phone in the other. He was calling the DART team—the Dangerous Animal Response Team.

I had to act fast. I smacked him again with my tail so he sprawled face-down in the grass. I shoved the phone out of his reach. Uncorking the bottle with my teeth, I poured the liquor over his head.

He rolled over and jabbed my leg with the cattle prod. My whole body felt like it was on fire. It hurt so much I couldn't move. Dunn stood up and jabbed my belly again. He was going to kill me.

A huge shape appeared behind Dunn. It was Austin! My grizzly bear brother had arrived to help me. He was standing on his hind legs, paws in attack mode. He towered over Dunn by at least three feet. The bear slammed Dunn to the ground and kicked the cattle prod in my direction.

"Run, Luke! The DART team is on its way!" he yelled. He shuffled back into the cave.

I grabbed the cattle prod and hurried as fast as I could back to the Reptile House. In minutes I was again in my glass enclosure. My back leg and belly were on fire where Dunn had jabbed me with the cattle prod. I was shaking from pain.

"What happened out there?" squeaked Megan.

"Shhh, I'll tell you later." I shoved the cattle prod under the straw and put my head down on the concrete floor.

Though they were several yards away, I could hear the DART team talking as they hunted the escaped Komodo.

Dunn was shouting at the top of his voice, "The Komodo is out! It stood up on its hind legs and jumped on me!"

"Which way did he go?" asked the night vet.

"That way! Toward the Reptile House!" yelled Dunn.

"The other guard is on the ground over here," said someone else.

"The Komodo attacked him, too!" Dunn was still shouting. "That animal is a killer! It needs to be put down."

Someone came to the door of the Reptile House. I opened one eye to see the night zookeeper. He looked in at me. I closed my eyes and didn't move. The zookeeper went back outside. I heard him talking to the others.

"The Komodo is in his cage, sound asleep. You smell like alcohol, Nikowski. Have you been drinking?"

No!" Dunn's voice sounded angry. "He poured it all over me."

A zoo golf cart pulled up. "I'm the night supervisor. What's going on here?" It was a new voice, one I hadn't heard before.

"Nikowski's been drinking," said the zookeeper. "He says the Komodo poured alcohol on him."

Everyone laughed. I almost felt sorry for Nikowski. Almost.

The night supervisor spoke again. "Did the other guard pour alcohol on you?"

"No, the damn Komodo did it," said Dunn.

"You're drunk, Nikowski." The supervisor's voice now sounded angry. "You know the rules. We don't tolerate drinking on the job. You're finished here. We'll send you home in a taxi. You can pick up your car and your last paycheck tomorrow. And you can tell your boss at the temp agency that we won't be hiring any more guards from him, either."

Their voices faded away. The zoo was quiet except for the occasional roar of a lion. The rain came down harder, splashing against the big windows of the Reptile House. Thunder rumbled somewhere in the distance. I felt cold and sick. My leg and belly screamed in pain where Dunn had stung me with the cattle prod. I was worried about my brother. I was hungry, too. I wished I was back in my own warm bed. More than anything, I wanted to be home. I wanted Austin to be there, too. It was hard to believe that we'd ever argued. That I gave him a bloody nose. Tears came to my eyes and dripped onto the floor.

"What happened out there?" said a small voice. I smacked my tail against the floor. In my haste to get away, I'd forgotten Megan's bag of food. I told her what took place.

The little red snake's head bobbed up and down as she talked. "It's okay. But if you go again tomorrow, maybe you could bring me some watermelon."

"We're getting out of here tomorrow. We'll get you and your uncle out, too."

I explained about the lightning striking the electromagnetic field and the Brockway family curse.

"Why would it fall on us? There isn't a curse on our family," said Megan.

"I'm not sure. But since you're here in the Reptile House, maybe it's because you were nearby when I changed form."

I heard steps outside.

"Hush," I whispered. "Someone's coming." I flattened myself down on the floor.

The door of the back room opened and the night veterinarian stepped in. He shined his flashlight on me.

"Dr. Hartley told me you have a burn on your belly, old boy. Let's have a look." He squatted down next to me. I rolled over on my back.

"Good boy!" said the vet. "If I didn't know better, I'd swear you could understand me." He shined the light on my belly and examined the marks. After a few minutes he stood. "There are two marks on your belly and one on your leg. They must be painful."

I flicked my forked tongue at him. I wanted to say they felt like fire, but I stayed quiet and tried to look pitiful.

The vet was talking to himself. "How on earth did this happen?" He stood up and looked around my enclosure. "There's nothing in here that could burn you." He stopped by the door and looked back at me. "How about a treat? Maybe a fat frozen rat. Or maybe some nice mice. Does that sound good?"

A tiny gagging sound came from the direction of the Death Adder's aquarium. I kept my teeth clamped together so I wouldn't laugh.

The vet went to the back room and reappeared with a few nice mice. He dropped them in front of me. "Old Dunn Nikowski said you poured alcohol on him. That's about the funniest thing I ever heard around here." He left, still chuckling.

When the night vet was gone, I pulled the cattle prod out from under the straw. Austin might need it when we made our break, so I had to get it over to him tonight. I rose up on my hind legs and slid back the bolt on my door.

"Where are you going?" The little snake's head bobbed up from the log.

"I'm just going to my brother's enclosure. I'll be back in a minute."

"If you see any watermelon, I sure would like some," said the Death Adder.

"All the trash cans are empty, but I'll see what I can find." I went out into the cold damp air for the second time that night.

Everything was still and silent. The night staff had returned to their buildings, and the place was deserted. I could see Austin sitting in his usual place at the front of the cage. He didn't like being near the other grizzlies. I didn't blame him. He was a lot bigger than they were, but they were real bears and Austin was just a eleven year-old kid with fur.

A few minutes later, I shoved the cattle prod through the bars to Austin. "Keep this handy in case you need it tomorrow."

"Thanks, Luke. If anything goes wrong, I just want to say I'm sorry. For everything."

"Stop that," I snarled. "You're getting out of here alive, and so am I. By this time tomorrow we'll be back in our own home, in our own beds. We'll have good stuff to eat."

"Toast with peanut butter?" Austin's tongue was hanging out. "Or maybe burgers and fries. And chocolate malts!"

"I'll take the money out of my piggy bank and buy you anything you want."

"Thanks, Luke." He was sitting up now. He took a deep, slow breath and smiled at me. He trusted me. I couldn't let him down. I had to make sure we all got out of here alive. And in human bodies.

I dropped down on all fours and shuffled away. There was a lot to do before morning. I still had to find Mr. Gifford and locate that watermelon for Megan. Where could I find watermelon? There were no farm stands or grocery stores in the zoo. The restaurant was closed. The trash cans were empty. Then I remembered the snack bar. It was across the park, near the African wildlife exhibit. I could check there for watermelon.

A vehicle was coming. I slid down into the shadow of a building and waited. It was the night guards in their golf cart. After they drove past me, I waddled as fast as I could to the African section of the zoo.

The rhinos were awake. I slithered along their enclosure fence, staying out of sight. One of the rhinos came over and sniffed at me through the fence. I backed away. I hoped their security fence didn't fail in the storm. If either of these guys got out, the DART team would need more than a couple of nets. They'd need tranquilizer guns. If the rhinos escaped into the neighborhood, the DART team would need real guns.

The hippo pond was in the middle of the African Veldt. A hippo stuck his head up from the water and opened his mouth very wide. That mouth was large enough to hold a pig. I wouldn't want to be there when those jaws snapped shut.

A lion lifted his head as I passed by. He flicked his tail the way a cat does when it's ready to pounce. Could a Komodo beat a lion in a fight? Probably not. If the fences around the lion's enclosure lost power, we'd all be in big trouble.

Three elephants, two females and a baby, stood together in the corner of the elephant exhibit. They seemed to be asleep. That was fine with me. I liked elephants, but I didn't know if they liked Komodo dragons.

So many dangerous animals were here in the zoo. The power to their security fences could go out during the big storm tomorrow. What would happen if the rhino and the hippo were free at the same time? And the lions and the tigers and other big cats? And the elephants and the grizzly bears? There were two or three DART teams, but it could take them a while to catch a big mammal. While they were going after one, two more could escape. They could wander into the nearby neighborhoods. They could eat the dogs and cats. They could eat anyone who happened to be outside. It wouldn't be pretty.

The snack bar was closed. It had a padlock on the door, but the padlock was broken. I removed it from the door and slipped in. There were burgers in the refrigerator, cooked but cold. I opened a bag with my claws and shoved in some burgers. After stuffing cotton candy, an apple and a fruit cup into another bag, I opened the door and peeked out. The night guard golf cart was headed towards the snack bar. I ducked back inside and crouched down on the floor.

A light flickered across the window once, and then again. They were checking the place with a flashlight. Luckily, they didn't notice the padlock was missing. Soon the golf cart pulled away. I huffed out a breath to calm myself. Then I grabbed the bags of food with my teeth. Keeping to the shadows, I hurried back to the bear cage and tossed the burgers and the apple to Austin. Back in the Reptile House, I dumped the fruit cup and cotton candy into Megan's glass cage.

"Where are you going now?" Megan's head wove back and forth above the log.

"I still have to find your uncle," I said. "If he doesn't know what to do tomorrow, he won't be able to change back into a human."

Megan didn't answer. She was burrowing into the cotton candy.

The Primate Forest was quiet. I let myself into the Ape House and looked around. A couple of big orangutans stared at me.

I asked, "Are either of you a human named Roy Gifford?" Neither of them answered.

I checked with the chimpanzees. "Are you Roy Gifford?" One of them scratched his head. The other one just stared at me like I was crazy. It was crazy, talking to Chimps. They talked to each other, but I didn't speak their language.

"Paging Roy Gifford," I called, walking back and forth in front of the cages. No answer. Great. Maybe he was on the Monkey Island.

"Looking for me?" said a voice behind me. I jumped and turned around. A Silverback gorilla faced me.

"Mr. Gifford?"

He crouched on the sidewalk, knuckles down. "Afraid so. Who are you? Your voice sounds familiar."

"I'm Luke Brockway. My brother Austin is here, too. Your niece is in the Reptile House." I explained about the Death Adder.

The Silverback got up, turned in a circle, and sat back down. "There isn't much I can do for her in this state." He looked me up and down. "What happened to you?"

"The same thing that happened to you. The important thing is, we're changing back into humans tomorrow." I explained everything. The Silverback listened, nodding.

"Stay out of sight until the storm hits. My grandfather will show up at dark to get us. As soon as night falls, come to the Reptile House. Wait outside, behind the brick fence. Don't let anyone see you. We won't leave without you."

Then I heard a familiar voice. It was the voice I never wanted to hear again, Dunn Nikowski's, from the parking lot. I kept quiet and listened. Dunn was talking to the guard who had passed me in a golf cart.

The night guard spoke. "What are you doing here, Nikowski? Why do you have a gun? If anybody sees you here, they'll call the police."

"I'm leaving," said Dunn. "But I'll be back tomorrow. No animal is going to make a fool out of me."

Chapter Six—Escape

"Luke, wake up!" Gramps was tapping on the glass. "Wake up. It's time!"

I pushed myself up on all fours and slithered to the back of the enclosure. I climbed up and undid the lock. "What time is it, Gramps?"

"A little after midnight. Let yourself out and I'll meet you behind the building."

My injured leg felt stiff. I blinked a couple of times to wake myself up. "We have to take Megan and Mr. Gifford with us, Gramps."

"Where are they?" Gramps glanced around. "We have to hurry!"

"Megan is in the corner snake enclosure. She's the Death Adder."

"Death Adder?" Gramps wiped the rain from his face and shook his head. "We can't take her. That snake's venom is fatal. We don't have time to locate the anti-venom serum."

"She won't bite us. We can't leave her. If she returns to her human self while she's in the aquarium with the real Death Adder, she'll be dead for sure."

I crawled behind the Death Adder's exhibit and tapped on the glass. "Megan, it's time. We have to go now." I slid back the feeding access door and put my right claw inside the aquarium where she could reach it. "Hop on. Just don't bite me, whatever you do."

"I'm afraid I'll fall," she cried. "Can you get any closer?"

I clambered up so she could slide onto my head. She was so light I could barely feel her weight. "Are you ready?"

"Ready," squeaked Megan. "Did you know you have red scales on top of your head?"

"Never mind about that. Just hang on. We have to get going."

I followed Gramps out into the rain. It was after midnight and most employees had gone home. The storm had started right when Gramps said it would. Thunder rumbled in the distance. The sky was turning green. The storm would be as bad as the one that changed us into animals. Lightning flitted and cracked across the sky, making a light show in the distance. The rain poured onto my back and ran down my tail. I blinked to flick the water off my eyelids.

"Mr. Gifford," I called. "Where are you?"

"Right here." He came out from behind the brick fence and ambled over to us.

Gramps put his hand over his heart. "You scared me. I didn't expect to meet a Silverback gorilla out here. How did you get out?"

The gorilla scratched his side. "I was never in. I've been hanging out here and there and searching for my niece."

"I'm right here, Uncle Roy," squeaked Megan.

The gorilla bent down to study my head. He started to reach for her.

"Don't touch her, Mr. Gifford. She might bite you by accident."

"I'm a Death Adder, Uncle Roy." She started to cry.

I flicked my forked tongue. "Stop crying, Megan. Gramps is going to tell us what to do."

"First we'll pick up Austin," said Gramps. "Stay together, next to the fence. Follow me." He took the lead, gesturing for us to follow.

With my forked tongue, I tasted the air for humans. No one was nearby, but there were still zoo workers who could see us if we weren't careful. We had no good way to hide an old man, a Komodo dragon with a snake on its head, and a Silverback gorilla—all moving along together in a group. So we kept to the shadows.

Now we just had to pick up my brother. I was a lot faster than the rest, so I hurried ahead to the grizzly area. Two big bears sat near the edge of the enclosure. Austin was nowhere in sight. I hoped he was okay.

"Austin," I called softly. "Austin, where are you? It's time to go!"

"Here I am." Austin lumbered out of the cave behind the grizzly bear exhibit. "I've been waiting for you."

Bunched together near the big bear cave, we checked for humans again. I couldn't hear anyone. There was no one nearby.

"Gramps and the others are waiting by the fence," I said. "Follow me."

I crawled to the nearest bushes. Austin got down on all fours and followed. We were both dark-colored animals, so we blended into the shadows. A few minutes later we arrived at the fence.

Austin nodded at the gorilla. "Are you Mr. Gifford?"

"The same." The gorilla offered his hand and the bear shook it.

The rain was rolling off Gramps' hat and down his neck. "Let's head for the parking lot. We want to be out of the zoo when the reversal takes place."

I shivered. The air was cold, and I was in a reptile body. Reptiles are cold-blooded, so my temperature was dropping as the air grew colder.

"When will it happen, Gramps? I'm freezing."

"Me too," said a tiny voice above my head.

Gramps bent over to peer at Megan, who was coiled on top of my head. "If you promise not to bite, I guess you could climb into my pocket." He held it open.

"Um...I'd rather not take any chances," said Megan. "If I can't see, I might bite you by accident. Could you just wrap that scarf around me?"

Gramps unwound the scarf from his neck and draped it over Megan. "Lift your head, Luke. I'm going to tie this under your chin."

Great. Not only was I a Komodo dragon, I was a Komodo dragon wearing a head scarf. How much more ridiculous could this situation get?

Lightning cracked overhead, hitting a wire. The wire sizzled and fell to the ground.

"It's starting!" yelled Gramps. "Start wishing you were human again."

"What if it doesn't work?" said Austin. His fur was wet, and he was shaking. I was afraid he was going into shock.

"Austin, you have to think the right thoughts, remember? Imagine being a boy again, like you were before. And don't think anything else." I turned to Gramps. "What about the lightning rod? Don't we have to take it up to the water tower?"

"No. I put metal poles near the main transformers. The lightning will be drawn to the poles. It should affect the electromagnetic field the same way it did before." He patted Austin on the back. "Start wishing, right now. All of you must want to be human, like before. Keep that thought in your mind no matter what."

We came upon a guard near the exit. Wet and cold, we huddled together behind some trees. "How did you get past the guard when you came in?" I whispered.

Gramps pointed to the wooden fence. "I went through the employee door. It's in the fence. We have to go out that way, too. I parked the car in the employee lot."

The guard opened his newspaper. He began reading, his head down.

"Now," whispered Gramps. "The guard isn't watching. Hurry!" He opened the door that led through the wooden fence to the employee parking lot. Austin held the door while Gramps and Mr. Gifford passed through. I slithered through the door with Megan still coiled on my head under the scarf. Austin had just closed the door when we heard a voice.

"Just the two I was looking for," said Dunn Nikowski. He stood with his legs apart, holding a heavy-looking rifle in his hand. He glanced at Austin, and then at me. "No animal is going to make a fool out of me."

He took aim, pointing the gun at me. Austin roared and swiped Dunn with his paw. Dunn fell backwards, and the gun fired. A branch fell from a tree above our heads.

A clap of thunder crashed so loud it seemed to shake the earth under our feet. Lightning struck barely a second later. The air around us started to whirl. The sky went from black to greenish yellow. The wind roared, bending the tree branches and knocking over the barricades in the parking lot. Things started to fly though the air; leaves and sticks and trash. Gramps' hat flew off and rose up into the sky. Gramps grabbed Austin's paw and hunkered down next to me. The gorilla tightened my head scarf to keep his niece from blowing away.

The earth started to sizzle around us. It was the same sound I'd heard before I became a Komodo dragon.

"Here it comes," shouted Gramps. "Get your thoughts straight. Wish you were human again, with your life just as it was. Wish the others were home again, too, just as they were before."

I was still thinking about Dunn. It was hard to switch my focus, but I had to do it. I wished as hard as I could to be myself again. I thought of how I looked in the mirror, red hair and all. Whatever. I didn't care, just so I was a regular guy. I wished Austin back the way he was before, good grades and all. Exactly as he once was.

"Hang on!" Gramps screamed over the roar of the wind. "Keep wishing!"

My skin tingled all over, like it was leaping off my body. I tried to find the car, but I couldn't see it. Everything was whirling around me, like a speeding merry-go-round. The air spun into a tornado of color, twisting sideways and forming a tunnel.

"You have to go through it!" cried Gramps. "Hurry!"

Austin disappeared into the twirling tunnel. The gorilla followed. Gramps was half in and half out, holding out his hand to me. I tried to grab it, but something was holding me back.

"Luke, take my hand," ordered Gramps. "Now!"

"Something's got my leg!"

"You aren't going anywhere," shouted a voice behind me. It was Dunn Nikowski. He was holding my legs so I couldn't follow Gramps. Gramps tried to pull him off me, but Dunn wouldn't release his grip.

I had to get loose! If I didn't, I'd be a Komodo dragon for the rest of my life. I kicked at him with all my might then reached down to claw him with my front nails. A red blur slid down my arm. Dunn let go. I heard him screaming as I tumbled into the whirling tornado.

"I want to be myself again," I cried. "Just like I was before. I want Austin to be himself, too!"

In the shrieking wail of the wind, I could hear Dunn Nikowski screaming, "Help! The Death Adder bit me!"

The wind died down. Things fell out of the sky as the wind dropped them. Gramps' hat fell to the ground next to him. A twig hit me on the head. I reached up and pushed it away. Then

I saw my hand. It wasn't a claw. It was a human hand. Austin was sitting on the ground next to Gramps. He looked pale and weak, but he was my brother. He wasn't a bear anymore. I was so glad to see him I almost cried.

Next to me, a tall man was brushing dirt from his jacket. "Megan, where are you?" He glanced around.

Megan wasn't on the ground beside me. She wasn't with Gramps or Austin. I couldn't see her anywhere.

"Oh no!" I cried. "Megan isn't here! She must still be in the zoo!"

We were standing in the employee parking lot. The car was only a few yards away. No one else was there. It would be easy to escape, but we couldn't leave without Megan.

"What happened to her?" wailed Mr. Gifford.

I tried to explain. "Dunn Nikowski was holding onto my back legs. Then he screamed that the Death Adder bit him and he let go. She bit him to save me."

"But where is she?" Mr. Gifford appeared frantic. "We've got to find her!"

I didn't want to tell him all the places where the wind could have blown her. She could have been tossed over the moat into the lion's enclosure. She could have landed in the hippo river, or on top of an elephant or in the wolf den. She could even be back in the exhibit with the real Death Adder.

We had to save Megan, but we had to care for Austin, too. He looked weak and pale from not having enough food for three days, and I didn't think he could survive another trip around the zoo.

"Maybe Austin should wait in the car, Gramps. He doesn't look so good."

"No. We'll stick together," said Gramps. "Remember, it might be very different in the zoo now."

The guard was not at the gate, so we crept quietly back into the main section of the zoo. Out of the shadows loomed a huge shape. It lifted its trunk and nosed at a tree.

One of the zoo employees saw it. He shouted to another employee, "The elephant is out! The power is off and the security fences aren't working. Call the DART team."

The elephant pulled some leaves from the tree and shoved them into her mouth. She seemed calm enough. The little elephant was out, too. He followed close behind his mother, waving his tiny trunk in the air.

Something big and furry crawled out of the cave behind the bear enclosure. It stood up on its hind legs and sniffed at the air.

"Oh no," whispered Austin. "It's one of my former roommates. I hope she doesn't recognize my scent."

"Stand still," I said. "Don't run or she might chase us."

We stood there, frozen, watching the big grizzly. She turned in our direction and dropped down on all fours. She then moved slowly toward us. Austin edged in front of me.

"Stand still," I said again. The bear looked at Austin. She seemed confused. Standing up, she sniffed the air again, got back down on four feet and meandered away.

I poked Austin's arm. "Why did you do that? You could have been mauled."

"I hoped she'd remember my scent and leave us alone."

I put my arm around his shoulders. "You probably just saved my life."

"Let's get out of here," said Gramps. "People are coming."

Zoo staff came from all directions, carrying big flashlights. The beams shined in circles that danced on the paths and in the trees. It looked like three different DART teams were searching for dangerous animals. I could hear them calling to one another. The night veterinarian seemed to be in charge. He called out his directions in a firm voice.

"There's a grizzly, right over there," said the vet. "Tranquilize it and call for the big lift."

One of the zoo security guards raised a gun. He fired. The bear turned toward the guard. Another zoo employee raised a tranquilizer gun, too. The bear sat down. Then it flopped to the ground with a thud.

"There's an elephant near the fence," said the vet. "Team two, get the elephant. What's next?"

"A guard saw the Komodo near the employee door," said a maintenance man. "And the Death Adder got out and bit Dunn Nikowski. They've given him the anti-venom shot and called the ambulance."

"Nikowski shouldn't have been on the grounds," said the night supervisor. "I fired him yesterday for drinking on the job. He must have let the Death Adder out of the aquarium. There's no other way it could have escaped."

"We'll sort Dunn out later," said the vet. "Right now we have to recapture the dangerous animals. Team three, look for the Komodo and the Death Adder. Check the area around the employee exit. And be careful. The Komodo is dangerous, but he's big enough to see. The Death Adder is tiny, but its venom is fatal."

"One of the lions is out," said the night nursery attendant. "I saw him sniffing around the hot dog stand."

I knew there were no hot dogs left, because I had eaten them all earlier in the evening. I hoped the lion wouldn't decide to snack on the humans in the area.

"Team one, as soon as they get the bear on the lift, go after that lion. The big cats are a priority. Shoot them if you must. We can't take a chance on someone being killed."

I didn't like hearing that. It would be bad if they had to kill any of the big cats. But I didn't want anybody to be eaten, either. Zoo animals look so calm in their cages that people forget how dangerous they are.

The DART teams went in separate directions.

"Let's go," I whispered.

Just as I stepped out of the shadows, a zebra went by in a black-and-white blur. It was so close I could have reached out and touched it. The lion was right behind the zebra. We hurried into a nearby building and slammed the door.

"Whew," said Austin. "That was close. I hope the DART team gets that lion before he catches the zebra."

I didn't answer. Something large and dark with a pointed nose growled softly, just behind me. It was a wolf. No, it was two wolves.

Gramps, Mr. Gifford and Austin stared at them.

"What do we do?" Austin's voice sounded full of fear.

"Shh. Wait." I could feel something coming from the wolves. Behind the growl there was a cry. They were afraid. I focused my thoughts on the wolves. *We won't hurt you. We're scared, just like you.* One of the wolves whined, but they didn't move.

"Everyone out," I said. "Walk, don't run."

The group backed out slowly. When Gramps and the others were clear, I turned to the wolves again, trying to send them my thoughts. *Leave the building and follow the fence to your enclosure. Hide in the warming shed. You'll be safer there.*

"Close the door, Luke," said Mr. Gifford, "or they'll come after us."

Sure enough, the wolves were leaving. But they didn't go after us. They went directly to the fence and started back to the wolf field. It had to be a coincidence. They couldn't have understood me. Maybe they just went because we left the door open.

Danger was everywhere. A large, blonde-colored cat stood on the pavement just ahead of us. A mountain lion! Mr. Gifford grabbed the trash can lids and banged them together. The cat loped off.

A giraffe walked by in its stiff-legged gait, tall and dignified. It stopped and nosed the top of the trees. I'd never been that close to a giraffe before. Any other day it would be fun to see one like this, but now we didn't have time. We were still about fifty yards from the Reptile House. If Megan was there, she was sure to be in danger. I wanted to run ahead, but Gramps stopped me.

"We don't know what we'll find there, Luke. Let's stay together."

The ground under us started to shake. It felt like the vibrations of a train. Something heavy was coming at a pounding gallop. We reached the Reptile House and slipped inside just in time. A rhino thundered past the door, a DART team right behind him. They were driving jeeps and trying to herd the rhino back into its space. In the passenger seat of both jeeps was a zookeeper with a tranquilizer gun. A third jeep pulled out around them. The man in the passenger seat had a high-powered rifle. I hoped he wouldn't have to use it.

"Let's find Megan," said Mr. Gifford. "We have to get out of here before they notice us."

"Or before something eats us," I muttered.

We left Gramps and Austin in the jeep, and Mr. Gifford and I went to the front door of the Reptile House. A loud crash made us both jump. I pushed the door open and peered inside.

"The big croc is out! Get back," I whispered. "We can go around."

Mr. Gifford wouldn't listen. "I have to find my niece." He pushed through the door and walked slowly toward the snake aquariums. I followed.

The big crocodile was across the room, lying very still on the floor. It was staring at a giant gray lizard. The lizard stared back, flicking its yellow forked tongue in the air. It was the Komodo dragon. It was outside its enclosure, too. The Komodo tasted the air again and stretched its head toward Mr. Gifford. He was staring into the Death Adder aquarium. It was empty.

"Mr. Gifford," I said softly. "She's not here. We have to leave. Don't move until I tell you."

I edged around the room until I reached the door to the back room. This put me within five yards of the Komodo. He turned his head, flicking his tongue. I raced to the freezer and pulled out an armload of frozen rats and rabbits. Holding the door open with my shoulder, I started pitching the frozen rats to both animals. The Komodo grabbed one and gulped it down. The croc didn't move. I threw him a rabbit. He swallowed it in one bite.

"Get out, now!" I shouted. I pitched the last two rats, one to each animal. "Go!"

I backed away so Mr. Gifford could get past me and followed him out the back door. The others were waiting for us outside the Reptile House.

Mr. Gifford was frantic. "Where is she?" he cried. "We have to find her."

Gramps put his arm around Mr. Gifford's shoulders. "She probably didn't change back, Roy. She's here somewhere, and we'll find her. Or they'll find her and return her to the snake exhibit. When they do, we'll rescue her."

"Right now we have another problem." I pointed to the shadows.

Just ahead of us, barely visible under the dim emergency lights, was the lion. The zebra must have gotten away from him. If that zebra was smart, it would leave the zoo and keep on going.

Where was the DART team that was sent to catch the lion? We stayed back where it was dark, but I was pretty sure the big cat knew we were there. What would we do if he charged? If I was still a Komodo, I could have protected the others. But now I was just a fourteen-year-old boy. I knew some Karate, but I couldn't stop a lion with a Karate chop. Would he like a few frozen rabbits? Or maybe some nice mice?

Gramps and Mr. Gifford stood like statues as they watched the lion.

"Gramps," I whispered. "There's a cattle prod in the Reptile House and a tranquilizer gun."

The lion turned his head. He was staring straight at us. A small animal scurried past him. Silky black, with a plumed tail. Wide, white stripe down its back. The lion roared. The skunk lifted its tail and sprayed.

"Let's get out of here!" exclaimed Gramps.

He hurried to the fence. Mr. Gifford followed him. Then I realized Austin wasn't with us. I scanned the area, but didn't see him anywhere. My heart began to pound. Where was he? He hadn't eaten much while we were zoo animals. He must have been too weak to keep up with us. Had one of the animals gotten him?

A motor churned softly, coming closer and closer. It was a golf cart, like the ones the security guards used. The cart pulled up next to us. Austin was in the driver's seat.

"Hop in," he called. "Let's go!"

"I'll drive," said Gramps. Austin slid over. The rest of us piled into the back and the cart took off. Behind us, the lion was wiping his face with a paw.

"Watch for a red snake," said Mr. Gifford. "Megan may try to find us."

He was upset. I didn't say anything, but I knew it would be useless to look for Megan now. The Death Adder was only twelve inches long. She couldn't move fast enough to locate us, and she was too tiny for us to see, especially in the dark.

We drove along the dimly lit route next to the Primate Forest.

"Are there any dangerous animals back here?" Austin sounded scared.

"The primates can be dangerous," I said. "Many of them are loose. We all need to keep our eyes open."

"There's another cart," said Gramps. "It's security. Everybody duck down. Maybe they'll think I'm one of them."

We all dropped down in our seats. The driver of the other cart was busy talking on his phone and didn't pay any attention to us.

It seemed as though we were on another planet. Overhead, monkeys chattered and swung across tree limbs. Another giraffe strolled past us, followed by her baby. The baby was about six feet tall. He stopped to nibble on the bushes. Birds of every size and color chirped and screeched as they flitted about our heads. The mountain lion leaped into the air, trying to catch one. It was a Disney movie gone haywire.

A downed wire lit up the dark road with red and yellow sparks.

"Be careful," Mr. Gifford warned. "Don't hit it."

Gramps had already spotted the wire. He drove far out and around it, and then back into the shadows.

"Other employees will be arriving to help with the emergency," said Gramps. "There will be heavy traffic in the employee parking lot. I hope we can get out before anybody sees us."

"We can't leave my niece here." Mr. Gifford sounded worried. "She'll be so frightened."

Five men were on foot in the road ahead of us. Three carried guns. They were part of the DART teams. Gramps quickly pulled behind a tree and stopped the cart so they wouldn't spot us.

One of the men was holding a small animal carrier and talking on a cell phone. "We found the Death Adder. It was in the employee parking lot. It bit Dunn Nikowski. We gave him the anti-venom serum before they took him to the hospital."

"At least we know she's okay," I whispered. "Don't worry, Mr. Gifford. We'll go back for her."

Mr. Gifford closed his eyes and turned his face away. His hands were clenched together. I wished we could rescue Megan, but too many people were in the zoo. Besides, she was still a snake. A very dangerous snake. She'd bitten Dunn Nikowski to make him let go of me. If it hadn't been for that, Megan would have gone through the twirling tunnel and I'd have been left behind. She'd saved me from a life spent in a zoo. Somehow I had to find a way to save her.

Gramps parked the golf cart near the fence. We followed him through the door and made it to our car without being sighted. Gramps stepped on the gas and the car jerked forward. We were on our way home at last. Then I noticed the cattle prod on the seat beside me. It made me think of the man who had used it on us. I hoped he didn't know where we lived.

Chapter Seven—Animal Traits

We were home at last! I flew upstairs and threw myself across my bed. The pillows were soft, the sheets and blankets smelled sweet and clean. I was dirty and I didn't smell very good. I got off my nice clean bed and went into the bathroom. The bathroom floor was wood, not concrete, and the room smelled nice and clean. I picked up the soap and sniffed it. It reminded me of pine trees. Running water felt wonderful on my hands. My fingernails were filthy. I picked up the nail brush and began to scrub.

Austin knocked on the bathroom door. "Are you taking a shower?"

"I was thinking about it." I picked up my toothbrush and studied it. I never thought I'd appreciate a toothbrush so much. It was beautiful. My teeth felt like they were covered with grit. I squirted toothpaste on the brush and began to clean my teeth.

"Let me know when you're finished," Austin said through the door.

"Use Mom and Dad's bathroom," I called back. "They aren't here, so they won't mind."

Fifteen minutes later we were both downstairs, squeaky clean and dressed in fresh clothes.

Gramps rubbed his hands together. "Let's order some food. Whatever you want—the sky's the limit! Pizza, burgers, milkshakes, or all of the above? Perhaps you would rather have eggs and bacon?" He eyed us, grinning.

Austin opened the refrigerator. "I wouldn't mind a tuna-fish sandwich."

I pointed to the pantry. "It comes in a can. Besides, I thought you hated tuna fish."

Austin pawed through the cans lining the pantry shelf. "I don't mind it so much anymore."

"How about you, Luke?" asked Gramps. "How about a pizza?"

Usually I liked pizza, but right then I didn't want any. "No thanks. Maybe later."

I went to the refrigerator and opened the freezer. No nice mice or frozen rats. It was filled with all the things I'd been wanting for three days. Chicken patties. Frozen fries. Ice cream. Blueberries. I picked up the box of chicken patties and handed it to Gramps. "How about some of these?"

"Whatever you want." Gramps took the box from me and placed four chicken patties on a baking sheet.

I didn't really care what we ate. I was just glad I didn't have to sneak around in the dark raiding trash cans to find food.

The chicken patties didn't taste very good. Austin was eating his second bowl of cereal with berries, tuna and honey on top. I pushed my chair back from the table and went into the living room. I turned on the large-screen TV we gave Dad for Christmas last year. An alligator was waddling across a golf course. At first it scared me. I thought the alligator had escaped from the zoo. But it was a Florida alligator, walking across a Florida golf course. The golfers waited until it moved off the green, and then went back to their game. I turned the TV off. I'd seen enough animals in the last three days. I didn't want to watch them on television.

Seeing that alligator made me think about the zoo. Megan was still there, trapped in that little aquarium. She was probably lonely and scared. Her uncle was going back to stay with her, but the zoo staff would make him leave when the zoo closed. Then she'd be there all alone, with only the other reptiles for company. Megan had bitten Dunn Nikowski so I could go through the whirling tunnel and become human again. Because of that, she'd lost her chance to become human. That was very brave. We needed to get back to the zoo and rescue her as soon as possible. I didn't like to think of her there alone.

I sniffed the air. Something was wrong. "I smell smoke, Gramps. Did you burn toast?"

"I don't smell anything," said Gramps.

Austin sniffed. "I don't smell anything, either." He poured berries on some tuna and made a sandwich.

"Something's burning!" I jumped up and ran outside. A strange smell wafted through the air. I raced down the sidewalk, following the smell. The odor was strange, as though a lot of different things were burning. Cloth, wood, plastic...all on fire, all at the same time.

There were no flames on our street, and the air on the next street was fine, too. But something was burning somewhere. The odor of smoke burned my nose. I kept going, following the smell. A few minutes later I passed the school, over a mile from our house. The smoke was still somewhere in the distance. A car pulled up behind me. Gramps was driving. Austin waved from the back seat.

Gramps put down the car window and called out, "You can't just take off like that without asking, Luke. Where are you going?"

"There's a fire somewhere ahead, and it's getting bigger. I can smell a lot more smoke now. We should call the fire department!"

"You ran a mile in less than five minutes," said Gramps. "I didn't know you could go that fast. You ought to train for the Olympics."

"It must have been an adrenalin surge," I muttered. I'd never been able to run fast before, at least, not as a human.

77

Komodos can run twelve miles an hour. Humans can't usually run that fast.

"Get in the car before the neighbors see you," said Gramps. "We'll keep the windows down so you can follow the scent."

I slid into the front seat and fastened my seatbelt. Gramps rolled down all the windows. I sniffed and told him where to turn. Five miles passed in ten minutes.

"I don't smell anything," muttered Gramps. "Luke, I think you're imagining this. You guys have been through a lot. You probably haven't recovered yet."

Austin crinkled his nose. "I can smell it now. Keep going."

We were almost downtown, in an area with mostly older homes. Some were boarded up. The smell of smoke was really strong.

"Here!" I yelled. "Pull over."

I jumped out of the car and flew up the steps of the nearest house. I could hear the crackle and pop of flames and the sound of wood cracking. I banged on the door, but no one answered.

"Gramps, call the fire department! Hurry!" I shouted.

Austin got out of the car and came to help. We both began to knock and shout. Lights went on in the house next door.

"What's going on out here?" A woman was standing on the neighboring porch. "Get out of here or I'll call the police."

"I smell fire!" I yelled. "Are there people inside?"

"Yes," said the woman. "An old man lives there."

Gramps left the car to join us. "The fire department is on its way. Let them handle it."

A faint voice cried out for help. Somebody was trapped inside the burning house. The house was locked up tight. I'd have to break a window.

"Somebody's in there. Austin, help me!"

Austin pulled back his fist and smashed the front door. The wooden door cracked and splintered. I stared at him. How could he break the door down with one punch? He'd never been this strong before. I'd never run a mile in five minutes before either, or smelled smoke that was miles away from our house.

I couldn't think about that now. Someone was inside the burning house, and we had to get them out. We stepped over the broken front door and went inside. The hall was thick with smoke. It was hard to breathe. I dropped to the floor where the air was better.

"Get down on the floor and crawl," I called to Austin. "There's more oxygen down here!"

"Help! Help!" The voice was weak and sounded far away. We crawled toward the voice. It was coming from behind another door. I yanked it open and almost tumbled down a stairway.

"This must be the basement. Follow me." I carefully took the steps, holding onto the wall to find my way. It was dark on the stairs, but I could see the fire ahead.

"Is anyone here?" yelled Austin.

Flickers of orange and yellow lit the darkness. The fire was here, in the basement. It was spreading fast, catching boxes and piles of newspapers. The floor was covered with hot water. A man crawled toward us. The side of his face had swollen into a big red blister.

"Help me," he whispered. "The boiler exploded."

"How are we going to get him out of here, Austin? He's too heavy to carry. We'll have to get help."

"No time."

Austin scooped the man up and threw him over his back. The man was a lot bigger than Austin, so his feet dragged on the floor. I followed Austin up the stairs, sniffing for fresh air. Smoke poured through the halls. My eyes burned and watered, and Austin started to cough. We had to get out of this building, fast.

Two men in fireman's gear burst through the door. Three more followed, pulling a hose. They took some of the weight off

Austin as they brought the burned man outside. Two paramedics raced over.

Gramps grabbed us both by the shoulders. "Into the car, both of you. Let's get out of here before anyone starts asking questions."

We jumped into the back seat. Gramps took off, winding around the fire engines, the rescue vehicles and a couple of police cars. In a few minutes we were away from the fire area and headed toward our own neighborhood. It took us about a half hour because the traffic was so congested. Everyone wanted to see the fire.

Gramps stared at me through the rearview mirror. "Six miles," said Gramps. "You smelled that smoke six miles away."

Austin leaned his head against the window. He looked the same as he had before we changed—same hair color, same height, and same face. Everything was the same, except Austin was now strong enough to break down a door with his fist. He was strong enough to pick up a grown man and carry him up the stairs and out of a burning house. He was as strong as a seven-hundred pound grizzly bear. And he was leaning his head against the window, which meant he was sad. He was a smart kid, and he'd already figured out what this meant.

Gramps glanced at me and then back at the road. "You were running twelve miles an hour. Do you know what that tells me?"

I knew, though I didn't want to admit it. Before being changed into a Komodo, I couldn't run around the block without getting winded.

"We retained our animal traits," said Austin. "We were animals just a couple of hours ago. Maybe they'll go away."

"Let's hope so. Or everybody is going to think we're freaks." I leaned my head against the window, too.

As we passed the pet store, I caught the scent of several animals—rats, rabbits and even some nice mice. They smelled good. I looked at Austin. He looked at me and licked his lips. He smelled something delicious, too.

Gramps parked the car in our driveway. He shut off the ignition and turned to us.

"Here's what I think. Let's forget about this, and try to go back to a normal routine. First, you guys need dinner. Then I have to write notes explaining why you've been out of school. We need to get our stories straight."

That night, I lay awake for a long time. Austin came into my room. He couldn't sleep either.

"What do you think happened to us, Luke? Do you believe we're still cursed?"

I sat up and turned on the light. "What else could it be? I could never run twelve miles an hour before."

Austin sat down on my bed. "If it doesn't go away, you could try out for track. You'd win all the meets."

"That would be different." I was terrible at sports. Austin was the athlete in the family. He was strong.

"You'll have to be careful, Austin. "You could accidentally kill somebody with that fist. Don't get mad and rip somebody's head off."

Austin's eyes filled with tears. "I don't want to be like this, Luke. That's why I quit Karate. I was afraid I'd hurt somebody. This is a lot worse. What if I can't control myself?"

I tried to cheer us up. "Like you said, we were animals just a few hours ago. Maybe it will wear off. In the morning we'll probably be our boring old selves again."

Austin hung his head. "But what if we're not? I don't want this freak-like strength. It was bad enough being super smart."

I didn't know he felt that way. "You don't like being smart?"

He shrugged. "Not especially. What good does it do?"

I could think of a lot of things. "You'll have an easier time in college. You can be anything you want when you grow up."

"I want to be like you," said Austin. "You know what's important."

I couldn't believe what I was hearing. My brother—who got straight A's and was the hero of the Lacrosse team—wanted to be like me. Why?

"Austin, I struggle in all my classes, except science. You're good at everything."

He shook his head. He looked sadder than ever.

"I know what's wrong with you. You're hungry. You haven't had enough to eat for the past three days. Let's go downstairs and get some grub."

Gramps ordered pizza. When it arrived, Austin dumped a can of tuna fish on his half. I ate mine with pepperoni and sausage. Usually that was my favorite. But now it didn't taste right. Afterwards we had ice cream. Austin poured honey and berries on his ice cream. I knew what I wanted on mine, but I didn't want Gramps to know. When the phone rang, he left to answer it. I went outside and caught a couple of bugs and a spider. I threw them on my ice cream and covered them up with chocolate syrup. It was pretty good, but it needed more bugs. Or maybe a couple of worms.

When the alarm went off the next morning, I dragged myself out of bed and got ready for school. When I went downstairs for breakfast, Austin wasn't there in the kitchen.

"Where's your brother?" asked Gramps. "I made pancakes. Go up and get him."

Austin was still in bed, fast asleep. I shook him gently. "Austin, get up. It's time for school."

He opened his eyes and pulled the covers over his head. "I'm so tired. I can't wake up."

"Gramps made chocolate chip pancakes. Aren't you hungry?"

"Hungry as a bear." He got out of bed and trudged into the bathroom. When I heard the shower running, I went back downstairs for breakfast. When Austin came into the kitchen, it was time to leave for school. His eyes were half closed, and he walked slowly.

"Here, Austin. You can eat these in the car." I handed him a plastic sandwich bag filled with three large, chocolate chip pancakes.

Going to school was a strange experience. When I opened the door, twenty smells hit my nose at the same time. The aroma of tacos wafted up from the school kitchen. Some girl out in the hall wore perfume, or maybe a lot of girls wore perfume. Somebody opened a stinky locker. It smelled like dirty gym socks. I never noticed so many odors before.

Austin and I went to the office to give the secretary the note Gramps wrote for us.

"You both had the flu?" The secretary studied my brother. "You still look pale, Austin. Maybe you should go home for another day. You don't want to get the other kids sick."

I stepped forward. "Maybe I should go home, too. I wouldn't want to make anybody ill, either."

The secretary peered at me over her half glasses. "I think you can go to class, Luke, but Austin needs to go home. I'll call your grandfather to pick him up."

The secretary gave me a paper for my teacher, and I headed for the eighth-grade classroom. Then I thought of something. If Austin and I still had animal traits, what was happening to Mr. Gifford? I had to find out.

The gym was a beehive of noisy activity. Kids were laughing and running and bouncing around. Some of them were doing summersaults on the thick exercise mats. Others sat on the floor, talking on cell phones or playing games on their iPods. When kids played with their electronics in class, the teacher usually took the phone or iPod away. But Mr. Gifford didn't seem to notice. He was squatting on the floor, digging leaves out of a lunch sack. He ate a few leaves, peered into the bag, then turned the bag upside down and dumped out a banana.

In the office on first floor, Mrs. Callahan was talking to her secretary. Even though I was on the second floor, I could hear their voices clearly.

"I'm going up to the gym for a minute," said the principal. "Megan isn't here again today. I need to see if Mr. Gifford is back."

This was not good. If she came up here and saw Mr. Gifford eating a banana while the kids ran wild, our gym teacher would be in big trouble.

I hurried to his side. "Psst. Mr. Gifford." He looked up, but his eyes were glassy. He didn't seem to see me. "Mr. Gifford!" I yelled. "It's Luke Brockway."

He blinked. "Luke. What are you doing in my class?"

"The principal is on her way up here." I glanced at the noisy group of kids.

Mr. Gifford scrambled to his feet. He handed me the lunch sack and blew his whistle very loud. The kids stopped running and throwing balls. They put their cell phones and iPods away. Everyone was quiet. I waved goodbye to Mr. Gifford and hurried back to the science lab. I made it just in time for class.

When I left school that afternoon, I had an armload of extra books and class-work we'd missed. I handed Austin his books, and we ate a snack. Austin wolfed down sardines with honey, and I had fruit. I thought about catching a nice fat squirrel, but I knew Gramps wouldn't want me bringing it into the house.

"I'm tired of sitting here." I got up and stretched. "Let's take a walk to the pet store."

Austin agreed. We didn't have any pets, but we liked to look at them.

The pet store was filled with enticing smells. Austin stopped at the fish tanks. He stood there for several minutes, watching the fish swim. I was bored, so I went to see the other pets.

Hamsters. Gerbils. White rats. Yum. Without thinking, I reached in and picked up a white rat by the tail. I sniffed it and opened my mouth.

"Can I help you, young man?" asked the sales clerk. She was frowning. "Would you like to buy that rat?"

"Um, I was just getting a closer look at it." I placed the rat carefully back in the glass aquarium and patted its little white head. "It has pink eyes. That's interesting."

"Yes." She narrowed her eyes at me. "Very interesting."

"Maybe I'll take an order of nice mice instead. Where are those?"

"An order of nice mice?" She rolled out each word slowly.

I was asking for an order of nice mice? I must be out of my mind. I pulled myself together. I was a normal kid now, not a rodent-eating Komodo. Besides, I hated those things when I was a Komodo. Why would I want to eat them now?

I backed away from the rat cages. "Thanks. I'd better find my brother."

Austin was staring into a tank of large fish. Suddenly he plunged his hand into the water and caught one. It wriggled in his hand, splashing water. I'd never seen Austin move that fast. One second he was looking into the fish tank, and the next second he had a fish in his hand. He raised the fish toward his mouth.

"What are you doing with that fish?" The sales clerk was next to me again. "Put it back, please. Customers may not touch the animals. If you want to buy a fish, I'll get it for you with a net." She did not look happy.

"Let's go, Austin," I whispered. "Gramps will be worried about for us."

"Why did we even go there?" asked Austin, as we walked home.

"To get pet food." I looked at my watch. Gramps would be wondering where we went.

Austin looked like he was waking up from a dream. "Pet food? But we don't have any pets."

I stopped and squinted at him. "I didn't want food for pets. I wanted to get pets for food."

His eyes widened. "You mean you were going to eat that rat?"

I had to admit, it was a disgusting thought. I hadn't eaten the rats Tim offered to me. Why would I want to eat them now? Yet I couldn't lie about it. A couple of nice mice on toast sounded good.

"Come on, Austin. That big fish was headed right for your mouth. If that sales clerk hadn't been there, you'd have swallowed it whole."

Austin stared at his shoes. "You're right." He sighed and shook his head. "We're still part animal. Sooner or later we're going to get into trouble over this."

When we got home, Gramps asked where we'd been. I took a deep breath and told him the whole story. He worked on supper while I talked.

"Is there any way to make these cravings go away?" I asked. "If I ask for an order of nice mice in the cafeteria, I'm going to end up in the principal's office."

"Or the school counselor's office," added Austin.

"I don't know. I'm not sure what's going on," said Gramps. He was making spaghetti sauce. It smelled delicious. I hoped that meant I was still mostly human.

"I think it has something to do with Dunn Nikowski," I said. "When I tried to get through that twirling tunnel, he grabbed my legs. I kicked at him, but he didn't let go until Megan bit him."

Gramps ladled spaghetti and sauce onto our plates. "Dunn didn't cause it. You lost your focus when you were trying to get away. What were you thinking when you felt him holding onto your legs?"

I thought back to that moment when we were trying to escape. Dunn grabbed me and held on. Then I remembered.

While Dunn was holding me, I wasn't wishing to be human again. I wasn't wishing for Austin to be human again. I was thinking, *"If I can't get away, I'll be a Komodo dragon for the rest of my life.*

Chapter Eight—Something Else About the Curse

We went back to school the next morning. I was in the science lab when I heard Jerry Magee's voice echoing up from the lower level. "Brockway," Jerry was saying. "Pick up your books. They're all over the floor."

My sensitive ears picked up the sound of grunts, then the thud of falling books. Magee was bullying my brother again. He wasn't going to get away with it this time.

I jumped up and sped down two flights of stairs. Then I tried to slow down so no one would notice how fast I could run. It was too late. They'd noticed. I could hear their comments.

"Who was that kid?"

"I don't know. He went by so fast his face was a blur."

"He should be on the track team."

I made it down two flights of stairs in just a few seconds. The hall outside the sixth-grade classroom was a mess. Papers and books littered the floor, trampled and kicked by kids who were trying to get to class. Nobody stopped to help Austin.

Jerry Magee was still there, leaning against the lockers. Every time Austin picked up a book, Jerry would knock it out of his hand. I'd told Austin not to hurt anyone, but this was ridiculous. I was at Magee's side in a flash.

His eyes popped open. "Where'd you come from?"

"Hell. And that's where you're going if you don't pick up those books."

"These books?" He kicked one with his foot and sent it sailing across the hall. It hit the wall and fell to the floor.

Austin walked across the hall and picked it up. "Ignore him, Luke. He's not worth getting in trouble over."

Magee grabbed Austin and lifted him, causing Austin to drop the book. I punched Magee's arm, causing him to drop Austin. He turned and glared at me. He was about three heads taller than Austin, and two heads taller than me. I didn't care. I wasn't going to let him get away with bullying my brother. I flicked my tongue at him.

Magee doubled up his fist and let me have it, right on the nose. It hurt so bad I saw black spots, and my eyes were watering. Something wet and red was coming from my nose.

The next second, Jerry Magee was airborne. He flew backwards just as the janitor passed by with a supply cart full of toilet paper rolls. Magee belly flopped into the cart. Rolls of toilet paper shot into the air and streamed across the floor.

"Get out of this wagon, right now!" screamed the janitor. "You're in big trouble, Magee!"

Mrs. Callahan, the principal, came down the hall in time to see Jerry climbing out of the supply wagon. He had a roll of toilet paper in each hand.

"Into my office, Jerry." She pointed to the top of the stairs.

"It's his fault!" Jerry jabbed a finger at Austin. "He knocked me into it!"

The principal adjusted her glasses. Her eyes moved down to Austin, and then upwards to Jerry. Jerry was at least a foot taller than Austin, and a lot more muscular. She rolled her eyes. "Sure he did. Into my office. Now!" Jerry still looked dazed as he dragged himself up the stairs.

Mrs. Callahan fluttered her hand at the large group of kids who'd stopped along the hall to watch. "Move along, children. The first hour bell rings in about ten seconds." Everybody disappeared.

"Want some help?" I picked up a handful of papers and gave them to my brother.

He stuffed them in his backpack. "I can handle it. You'd better get to class." He offered me a tissue. "Your nose is still bleeding."

It had to be said. I cleared my throat. "I'm glad Jerry hit that wagon full of soft toilet paper rolls. If he'd hit the wall he could have broken his neck." I dabbed my nose with the tissue.

Austin pulled on his backpack. "I was in control. I aimed for the cart. It was like kicking a soccer ball into the net." He smiled. "It felt good. Don't worry. I won't do it again."

I went into the bathroom and draped a wet paper towel over my nose. When the bleeding stopped, I washed my face and hands. By the time I got to the science lab, Mr. Riggs, the teacher, was just closing the door. I slipped under his arm and took my seat.

"Today we're going to talk about the electromagnetic field," said Mr. Riggs.

"What's that?" asked a girl in the front row.

"It's a field where they grow magnets," said the boy next to her.

Mr. Riggs leaned against his desk. "In 1964, Scottish physicist James Clerk Maxwell discovered some facts about electricity and magnetism. They turned out to be two parts of the same thing—the electromagnetic field."

He talked about light waves, sound waves, radio waves and microwaves. He talked about energy. But he didn't talk about how they could get mixed up during a lightning strike. He wouldn't know about our family curse, or how to get all those electromagnetic wave particles back where they belonged. I paid attention and took notes. Maybe I could learn something that would help us get rid of these lingering animal traits. Besides, I had to keep my A in science. Unless things changed, it would be the only good grade I got.

That evening, Gramps ordered burgers, fries and chocolate shakes. Austin went into the pantry and came back with a jar of honey and a spoon. He dug out a spoonful of honey and put it in his mouth. Gramps and I stared at him.

"I'm hungry," said my brother. "I've been hungry for days."

"You need protein, not sweet stuff. Get a can of tuna." Gramps nodded toward the pantry.

Austin dumped four cans of tuna fish into a bowl and spooned honey on top.

"You want whipped cream and nuts with that?" asked Gramps.

"Sure." Austin went back to the pantry and found a can of peanuts. He upended the whole can of nuts on top of the honey. Then he opened the refrigerator and found the whipped cream. He squirted a big pile of whipped cream onto the nuts.

I picked an onion off the top of my burger and squirted on some whipped cream. "We aren't back to normal yet, Gramps."

"Really? I hadn't noticed." Gramps poured ketchup on his fries. "Actually, I did notice one thing. You're better behaved than you were before that trip to the zoo."

Austin put his fork down. "Do you think we should try again? Go back, I mean?"

I put my burger down. It tasted awful. Maybe I should try one with cheese and sliced rabbit. "Austin is right," I said. "We have to go, Gramps. We have to get Megan."

Gramps nodded. "The weather is supposed to be bad again on the weekend. We can return then."

"Why did Mr. Gifford and Megan change into animals, Gramps?" I asked. "They aren't part of our family, so they shouldn't be under our family curse."

Gramps helped himself to another burger. "I don't know."

"Maybe you could go on Ancestry and look up our family tree," suggested Austin.

I threw the burger in the garbage. "Megan is still cursed. We have to help her." I looked at Gramps. "What about me and Austin? What if going back there doesn't make us better? I'm afraid we'll end up worse than ever."

Gramps pushed his plate away and sat back in his chair. "It's true. You could wind up worse."

That scared me. "What do you mean?"

He stood and began to clear the table. "We have to make sure Dunn Nikowski isn't around. You'd be a lot worse if he shot you dead."

The next morning, it was cold outside. I wore a sweater and a sweatshirt under my coat. Austin wore a tee shirt and no coat. I went to my locker on the second floor, and he went downstairs to his. About a minute later, I heard him cry out.

"Oh, no!"

I hurried down two flights of stairs to find Austin searching through his backpack.

"What's the matter?"

"I forgot my math homework. I must have left it at home. Mrs. Thompson will give me an F."

I looked at my watch. We had ten minutes before class started. "I'll get it. I'll meet you back in your classroom."

"You won't make it," said Austin. He yawned so big I could see his back teeth.

Austin could have made it home and back before his class started. Grizzly bears can run a lot faster than Komodos. Unfortunately, this one was hibernating. He yawned again, leaning against his locker.

"Austin, you have to go to class." I shook him.

"Oh, okay." He shuffled into his classroom and plopped down.

I ran as fast as I could. The school was about a mile from our house. It took me about five minutes to get home.

Gramps looked up from his newspaper. "Luke! What are you doing here?"

"Austin forgot his math homework." I tore up the stairs and rifled through the papers on his desk. I found the math paper, flew down the stairs and was out the door as Gramps pushed himself up from his chair.

"Here it is." I slapped the math paper on Austin's desk five minutes later. His teacher stared at me. "My brother's homework," I explained. "We studied together last night, and it got mixed in with my papers."

"Thanks," whispered Austin. "I owe you one."

The building was so cold. I went back to my locker to get my jacket. I could hear teachers talking in several classes. Mrs. Thompson called Austin's name. He didn't answer. That was odd.

I went downstairs and peeked into his classroom. All the students were busy writing, except Austin. My brother's head was on his arms. His eyes were closed. He was sound asleep!

Mrs. Thompson walked from the front of the room to his desk. "Austin, are you finished with your test? Austin?" She put her hand on his shoulder and shook him. "Austin, are you feeling okay?" His head came up, and he blinked. He looked confused.

The bell rang. It was the last bell for first hour. I should have gone to my first-hour class, but I stayed to see if Austin needed help.

Mrs. Thompson was frowning at him. "This isn't like you, Austin. Usually you pay attention in my class."

"I know." Austin looked sad.

"You've already missed two days of school and you haven't made up the work yet. Do you want to fail this class?"

Anger roiled up inside me. I gritted my teeth so I wouldn't flick my tongue at the teacher. She didn't know what Austin and I had endured the past week. It was a miracle Austin was in school at all.

"I know you were out sick," she said. "Maybe you need to stay home until you feel better. Go to the office and call your grandfather. I'll let them know you're coming."

Austin gathered up his books. I walked with him to the office.

"I can't stay awake, Luke." He rubbed his eyes. "What am I going to do?"

We told the school secretary Austin was still sick. She called Gramps to come get him. We sat on a bench outside the office to wait for Gramps.

"Mr. Gifford," said the principal. I looked around. The principal was nowhere around. Her voice was coming from her office, next door. She sounded upset.

"I know you're worried about Megan," said the principal. "She's been out sick all week. But this can't go on. When I went down to the gym this morning, the kids were running wild. You were sitting in a corner, eating bananas. I'm giving you a leave of absence. You need to see a psychologist."

I wanted to help Mr. Gifford, but what could I do? If I told the principal what really happened, she'd send me to the psychologist with Mr. Gifford. This was bad. Mr. Gifford would have to go back to the zoo with us. We all had to get rid of our animal traits. We also had to find Megan so she could become human again.

After school, I told Gramps what happened. He turned on the television and we watched the weather reports. Severe storms were traveling across the country, causing floods and tornados. The storms would hit our area on the weekend. Until then, there was nothing we could do. We'd have to try not to hurt or scare anyone.

I did my homework and then played games on my computer. Austin was on the floor in front of the television. He was sound asleep. His favorite show was on, but I didn't wake him up. He probably hadn't gotten much sleep at the zoo. Who could sleep with two grizzlies curled up ten yards away?

The phone rang. Gramps answered it and talked for a minute.

"He's feeling okay as far as I know," said Gramps. He listened then glanced at Austin. "He's sleeping now, as a matter of fact. He missed a test? That's not like him. Yes, I'll take him to the doctor. Thanks for calling."

Gramps came into the family room and looked down at Austin. He bent down and touched Austin's forehead.

"He doesn't seem to have a fever." Gramps shook my brother gently. "Austin, wake up."

"What?" Austin sounded crabby.

"I think I know what's going on," I said. "It was cold today. Bears hibernate when it's cold."

Austin groaned. "Another bear trait?" He yawned. Without another word, he climbed up on the sofa and went back to sleep.

I was worried. "What's going to happen? Will he fail the class?"

"The teacher said she'd let him retake the test. If he fails the test again, he can't stay in advanced math."

"He loves that class."

"I know." Gramps sighed.

I couldn't let my brother fail. He was a good student. It wasn't his fault he kept falling asleep. I couldn't go around flicking my tongue at people either. This morning I'd had to clamp my teeth together to keep from taking a small bite out of Austin's math teacher. Something had to be done before we got into serious trouble.

The next morning, Austin didn't come down to breakfast. I went upstairs to get him. He wasn't in his bed. He wasn't in the bathroom or the kitchen. He wasn't watching television in the family room.

"Where could he be?" Gramps scratched his head.

"He's probably sleeping somewhere—somewhere we haven't searched," I said.

We went back upstairs together. I looked under Austin's bed. Gramps looked in his closet. We checked the other bedrooms and the other closets.

"Maybe he's in the basement," said Gramps.

I shook my head. "He doesn't like it down there. It scares him. He says it's as dark as a cave."

Gramps eyes met mine. We were thinking the same thing. Bears usually hibernate in caves.

Gramps sighed. "You go get him. I'll make the toast."

There was an old sofa in the basement, and an old television set. Mom kept extra blankets, pillows and our old toys in the basement closet. Now all the old toys and games were piled on the floor outside the closet. I opened the closet door. There on the floor, in a den made of pillows and blankets, was my brother. He was snoring.

I shook his shoulder. "Wake up, Austin. Breakfast is ready. Gramps made you a nice bowl of tuna fish and berries."

"With honey?" Austin started to wake up.

"Lots of honey."

Gramps had our cereal waiting for us. Austin started to eat. Then he yawned and put his head down on the table. He was sound asleep again.

I couldn't swallow my cereal because my teeth were chattering. I'd put on two sweaters and a sweatshirt, but I was still shivering. I added my coat and pulled a hat down over my ears.

My cereal looked too plain. Maybe it needed a couple of nice mice.

Gramps put his hand on my forehead. "No fever, but you're not eating. Something's wrong, Luke. You'd better go to the doctor with us."

We climbed into the car and Gramps covered both of us with a blanket. Austin didn't notice. He was sound asleep.

When we arrived at the doctor's office, Gramps woke Austin up. We each took one of Austin's arms and half-carried him inside. The doctor checked our eyes, our ears, and our throats.

"They seem fine to me," said the doctor. "Luke's temperature is a little low. Austin's pulse is a little slower than usual. Keep an eye on them and call me if anything new develops."

When we got home, Austin went upstairs to bed. I was too cold to go upstairs. I kept my coat and gloves on.

"I'm freezing, Gramps. Could we build a fire?"

He made a fire, laying out the wood the way we did at Boy Scout camp. The flames crackled and danced, sending out waves of warm heat. I stretched out in front of it, basking like a lizard in the sun. I stayed there all night and all the next day. There was nothing else I could do. Every time I moved away from the fire, I started to shiver.

When we were at the zoo, we couldn't wait to get home. Now we were home, and everything had gone wrong. My brother couldn't wake up. I was spending my life on the rug in front of the fireplace. Neither of us could go to school. People food didn't taste good to us. We couldn't see our friends. We were failing our classes. What kind of life would we have without an education? We were home from the zoo, but we were more cursed than ever.

Our parents would be home soon. We couldn't let them find us like this. We'd never be able to explain it. Finally, I shared my fears with Gramps.

"We can't live like this, Gramps. We can't just lie around the house all day. What about our friends? What about our grades? Austin isn't a bear. I'm not a Komodo dragon. We're boys. We want to be normal kids again."

"There's only one thing left to do, I guess." Gramps stared at the floor.

Austin yawned. "We have to go back to the zoo."

Gramps nodded. "Yes. We have to go back. We have to rescue Megan. You boys need to get rid of your animal traits. But I don't want you guys to have to go through that again."

I didn't understand. "Go through what, Gramps? There's no other way to undo this curse, is there?"

"Let's talk about it after dinner," said Gramps. "Then we'll try to make a plan."

Dinner was rabbit stew with berries and honey for dessert. I ate the stew and Austin ate the dessert. Just as we finished our meal, the doorbell rang. It was Mr. Gifford. Gramps had called him to ask if he'd join us in formulating the plan.

Mr. Gifford sat down at the table. Gramps found a pen and paper and opened his zoo map.

"Here's the Reptile House." Gramps tapped the map with his pen. "Roy, you and Luke will go inside and grab your niece. Bring an empty shoe box. You'll need to hide her until she transforms back into a girl. If all goes well, we should be in and out within a half hour."

"What if it doesn't go well?" I asked. "What if Megan doesn't revert back?"

Gramps rubbed the back of his neck. "She's not the one I'm worried about."

"Are you worried about us?" asked Austin.

"Yes. There are some things I haven't told you about this curse," said Gramps.

I glanced at Austin. He rolled his eyes.

99

"You each still have some lingering traits," said Gramps. "That's because you aren't completely free of the curse. You can still become animals again when it's stormy. You'll have to do that when we're at the zoo."

Austin frowned. "Why would we want to change back into animals? We hated being animals."

Gramps shrugged. "It might help while we're there."

I didn't understand. "We don't have to turn back, do we?"

Gramps shook his head. "No, you don't have to, Luke. But each time you change, you get better at it. You make a cleaner break with the animal when you become human again. That helps you leave the animal traits behind." I felt better after hearing that. I'd gladly change into an animal if that would get rid of the rest of the curse.

Gramps held up a finger. "I promised I'd tell you how this started. It's a long story and we don't have time for all of it tonight." He poured Mr. Gifford a cup of coffee, then sat down at the table with us.

"Dunn Nikowski and I knew each other a long time ago, when young. We were in the Navy together, stationed in the Pacific. One day we took a trip to a nearby island, to see the Komodo dragons."

"Did you see any Komodo dragons?" asked Austin.

"Yes," said Gramps. "The place was covered with them. There were Komodo dragons everywhere. On the beach, in the jungles, on the rocks. Everywhere. Because of this, I had special permission to carry a gun." He sipped his coffee, and then continued. "They told us not to get too close to the Komodos, because they could attack humans. But Dunn didn't listen. Even then he had this idea that he should have power over any animal. If they didn't obey him, he'd kill them. He got too close and poked a Komodo dragon with a stick. It turned around and bit him on the leg. It didn't let go and I had to shoot it. The smell of blood brought more Komodos. We hurried to the jeep and got out of there, fast.

"Dunn was losing a lot of blood. I tied a tourniquet around his leg but he couldn't move. I took him to the only hospital on the island. They put him in a room and did what they could to treat him. He lost his leg, but they saved his life."

I sat up straight. "So that's why he walks so funny. He has an artificial leg."

"Yes," said Gramps.

"What happened after that?" asked Austin.

"The people were very angry. The Komodo I killed was one of the rare, pink Komodos of special importance to the people of the island. They believed that killing the pink Komodo meant they'd have bad luck for several years.

"A medicine woman and her daughter came to see Dunn while I was in the room. He had a high fever and didn't know what was going on. The medicine woman bent over him and placed a necklace around his neck. A painted shell hung from it, of a Komodo dragon. Then she waved a stick over my head and muttered words I didn't understand. I complained to the nurse in charge about the medicine woman and her ceremony in Dunn's room. The nurse just laughed.

"I never saw Dunn again until the other day in the Reptile House. I don't think he recognized me, but he threatened you guys. We'll have to go back to the zoo. He could still be there, waiting for us. We have to be ready for him."

"He wasn't one of the zoo's regular security guards," said Austin. "He was a temporary employee. He was only there because they needed to train the new guards."

Gramps waved his hand at us. "That's enough for now. Go to bed. You need your rest. Tomorrow we'll go back to the zoo."

Austin staggered up the stairs. I walked behind him to make sure he didn't fall. When he was safe in his bed, I headed to my room. While I got ready for bed, I recalled all that Gramps told us. He said Dunn Nikowski might still be after us. If he showed up with a gun again, we might need a weapon, too. I took the cattle prod from the back of my closet and propped it up next to the door so I wouldn't forget it when we left for the zoo. It wasn't much, but it was better than nothing.

I crossed the hall to the bathroom, tasting the air with my tongue. The air tasted like tuna fish and human sweat. I felt so strange. What was wrong with me? I leaned over the sink and stared at myself in the mirror. A pair of bright yellow eyes gleamed back at me.

Chapter Nine—Treasure Hunt

We were the only people in line when we arrived at the zoo. It was cold and rainy. I wished I was home, wrapped in blankets and basking in the warmth of the fire. I hunkered down in my parka and glanced at the sky. Heavy clouds hung over the zoo like clumps of gray cotton candy. Cold rain drizzled down my neck. I pulled up my hood and tied it tight under my chin.

Gramps showed his pass to the lady in the ticket booth.

"The zoo is closing in fifteen minutes, sir," she said.

He nodded. That was exactly what we'd planned. Most of the visitors were already gone. The staff was busy feeding the animals. We planned to stay out of sight until everyone left. Then we'd go find Megan.

We followed Gramps through the gate. The rain slammed against the pavement, splashing us. I hunched further into my parka, shivering. The cattle prod was under my coat. If we didn't need it, I'd leave it in the Reptile House.

Austin dragged behind us. "I hate this place," he mumbled.

Gramps looked sad. "You used to love the zoo."

"That was before I spent three days as an exhibit." Austin yawned.

"Let's go to the Reptile House," said Mr. Gifford. "Megan is waiting for us."

He was wrong. Megan was not waiting for us. The Death Adder's aquarium was empty. There was no sign of Megan. The Komodo paced behind the glass, flicking his forked tongue. The crocodile crawled out of the water and slapped his tail on the concrete. The frogs shrieked like they were being attacked. The snakes burrowed under the sand or hid in logs. Fear oozed over the Reptile House like fog.

A shadow slid past the outdoor section of the Reptile House. I peered out there, but I couldn't see anyone. It must have been my imagination.

"What do we do?" asked Mr. Gifford. "How can we find her? Will she become a girl again when lightning strikes?"

"Well, not exactly," said Gramps. "There's something else I haven't told you about this curse." Austin and I groaned.

"Gramps, why didn't you tell us last night?" I cried. "How much more is there?"

"You guys were too tired to hear any more about the curse," said Gramps. "You needed a good night's sleep."

The storm arrived. Thunder crashed and rolled like giant bowling balls over our heads. Rain clattered on the roof and rattled the windows.

Gramps voice rang out. "There's a shelter down by the hippo pond. Let's go there."

We followed him, hurrying through the rain. The gate to the hippo pond was open. Wind whipped the water up onto the muddy banks. We had to reach that shelter so we could talk without getting soaked. Gramps still hadn't told us the last part of the curse.

"Stop right there," snarled an angry voice. "I've been waiting for you." Dunn Nikowski emerged from the shadows, holding a gun.

"I told you we'd meet again," said Dunn. He glared at Gramps. "You thought I didn't recognize you, didn't you. Like I could forget what you did to me. Because of you, I have a tin leg." He sneered at me and Austin. "I'm glad you're all here together. I'll get rid of you all at once."

"Leave them out of it." Gramps stepped in front of us. "It's between the two of us. It was a long time ago, Dunn."

Dunn waved the gun in the air. "You left me on that island to die!"

"I took you to the hospital, Dunn. I put a tourniquet on your leg. I saved your life."

"You lie!" Dunn shoved the muzzle of the gun into Gramps' chest.

Lightning cracked and splintered across the sky. I caught Austin's eye, and he nodded. Neither of us knew what had happened between Dunn and Gramps, but it didn't matter. Gramps was in danger. Austin and I could protect him better if we were animals. It was time to change.

Closing my eyes, I wished as hard as I could. It was easier this time. Energy zipped through me. My body quivered. The cattle prod fell to the ground. My arms and legs shortened and grew scales. As I lay sprawled on the ground, my hands and feet became claws. I slithered forward, flicking my forked tongue, and grabbed Dunn's leg.

Austin was bigger than ever. His furry body reared up to a height of ten feet. He brought his paw down hard on Dunn's head.

Dunn crumpled to the dirt. At first I thought Austin had knocked him out. But then something strange occurred. Dunn started to roll. He tumbled and stretched and grew longer. Scales sprouted all over his body. He rolled again, growing so heavy he made the ground shake. His head flattened out into a long, heavy snout. Bulges formed over his eyes. Sharp, ugly teeth projected from his upper and lower jaws. Dunn Nikowski had morphed into a gigantic crocodile! He was over twenty feet long, and probably weighed two thousand pounds.

This was what Gramps was going to tell us. He and Dunn had been on that island together. They were both cursed. If we could change into animals, so could Dunn.

Dunn was bigger than the giant crocodile in the Reptile House. He roared and snapped his huge jaws. I shrieked in pain. He had my leg! I struggled, but I couldn't get away. He dragged me across the dirt and into the hippo pond. He sank under the water and began the death-spiral. I turned with him, plunging lower and lower into the cloudy green water. My nose and eyes filled with water. I paddled frantically with my front claws. I was drowning!

Something huge and dark dived into the water. Furry legs kicked the water in front of me. It was Austin, my grizzly bear brother! Dunn let me go, and snapped his powerful jaws on Austin's leg. He rolled again, taking Austin down and under. The croc was bigger than my grizzly bear brother.

I bobbed to the surface, screaming. "Gramps! We can't take him! He's too big!"

Gramps yelled back, "A hippo! A hippo could take him!"

Squeezing my eyes shut, I saw a giant hippo in my mind. My body shuddered. My short legs grew, pounding the water around me. My body exploded into five tons of quivering muscle. My head grew long and wide. My body was slick and rounded. I slid through the water like a ten-thousand-pound otter.

Austin's furry head went under the water again. I opened my enormous mouth and aimed for Dunn's midsection. One snap would break him in half. Good riddance.

He turned, churning the water around us. My jaws crashed together, but all I got was a mouthful of water. I sank, searching the depths for a sign of him. Austin was moving slowly toward the shore. Dunn was gone.

Austin and I crawled out of the pond. I was so confused. This was all happening too fast. Where was Dunn now?

"Look out!" cried Gramps.

Dunn was next to us, human again. His eyes glowed red in the darkness. Then his body quivered and fell. He twisted in the dirt, thinning like a ball of play dough when you're rolling it under your palms. When he stopped moving, he was at least sixteen feet long, olive-green with pale yellow rings. He was a snake. A very big snake. He was as long as a python, but he wasn't a python. He wasn't a boa constrictor, either. The front of his body reared up, glowing red eyes still fixed on me. His neck spread out into a hood. He hissed and spat. Now I knew what kind of snake he was: a gigantic Egyptian cobra.

"Be careful," warned Austin. "Cobra venom is deadly."

"He'll have to get those fangs through my hide." I inched forward, ready to trample the snake.

The others were ready to help. Gramps aimed the cattle prod at the back of the snake's neck. Mr. Gifford held up a heavy rock, ready to smash it on the snake's head. Austin stood next to me, paws apart.

The cobra hissed, red eyes glowing like embers in a fire. It twisted around, eying each of us in turn.

"You might kill me," he hissed, "but I'll take two of you down with me." He turned in a circle, whipping his tail through the dirt. "Which two will it be?"

I opened my huge jaws, ready to snap him in half. He turned, and I turned with him. He wasn't getting away from me.

The cobra weaved back and forth as it spoke. "I've hidden the Death Adder away. If you kill me, you'll never find her." He twisted, flipping his snake body through the dirt with blurring speed. A screeching laugh rang through the air. "I'm a fair guy," hissed Dunn. "I'll give you an even chance. We'll have a little treasure hunt. I've even left clues to help you find her."

Mr. Gifford groaned. The gigantic snake whipped around, looking down on him. "You'll find the first clue in the seal pond." With lightning speed, the snake disappeared.

107

Austin and I changed back to our human forms. It was so easy to change now. All we had to do was think it. We didn't need the lightning. We didn't even need a storm.

"What's going on, Gramps? Why is it so easy to morph?"

"That's what I was going to tell you," said Gramps. "But I didn't have time. Here's the seal pond." He lowered his voice to a whisper. "Get back. The zoo keeper is there."

We hid behind a hedge and watched. The keeper slid a large disk of ice out onto the seal pond. Inside the frozen disk were three fish.

"They have to get the fish out of the ice," I whispered. "It keeps them from being bored."

The seals darted through the water like missiles, aiming for the floating ice disk. Two of them smacked into each other, then dove under the water. In seconds they emerged again, shaking their whispers. They nosed the round pad of ice. The keeper watched them for a minute, then left.

"Where's the clue?" Mr. Gifford peered over the fence.

Austin pointed at the water. "There's something floating in the pond. It looks like an egg."

"It's one of those big plastic Easter eggs," said Gramps.

"Plastic can choke animals," I cried. "We've got to get it out of there, fast."

One good thing about the rain—nobody else was out in it. I climbed the fence and stood on the edge of the pool. I took off my coat and handed it over the fence to Gramps.

"See if this will reach it." Gramps gave me a long stick.

I extended it out as far as I could over the water. I almost had the egg. I pushed the stick a little farther. My sneakers slipped on the slimy, wet concrete, and I splashed face-first into the seal pond. Bits of seal poop floated past me. I turned away in disgust. The depth was over my head. I treaded water for a minute, in search of the egg. Then I spotted it, floating nearby.

One of seals barked and swam toward me. I didn't know if he wanted to play or if he was protecting his territory. One thing I knew for sure—he was a much better swimmer than me.

I grabbed the egg and paddled as fast as I could toward the edge of the pond. A long, slick body hit me in the back, knocking me under. I swam up toward the surface, but the seal pushed me beneath the water again. My lungs felt like they would explode. I couldn't hold my breath any longer.

Something long and narrow snaked around my waist. It lifted me out of the water and up into the air. Gasping for breath, I landed in the dirt at Gramps' feet. An elephant's trunk swayed back and forth in front of my eyes.

I squinted up at the elephant. "Where did you come from?"

"I'm not sure," said Austin. "All I know is that I wanted to save you. I wanted to grab you and pull you out of the pond. Before I knew what was happening, I was an elephant."

"That's what I tried to tell you before," said Gramps. "Change back, quickly! If someone sees you like that, they'll call the DART team."

The Austin-elephant stood very still. It began to tremble, shaking the earth beneath our feet. His gray hide blurred then melted into the pouring gray rain. The elephant disappeared. Austin stood there, soaking wet and shaking.

I was shaking too, from the cold. I rubbed my arms, complaining, "Why didn't I just wish to be an eagle? Then I could have swooped down and grabbed the egg without getting wet." The words were hardly out of my mouth when I felt the prick of feathers growing under my arms.

"No! No! Not now!" I cried. "I want to be a kid again. I want to be a kid!" The prickling stopped. The feathers melted away.

Gramps handed me my parka. "That was close. Be careful what you wish for, Luke."

Gramps rubbed his chin. He opened his mouth as though he had more to say. I waited, but Gramps didn't say anything else.

Had he told us everything about this mysterious curse? I had the feeling he was holding back. There was something he wasn't telling us. There might be a lot of things he wasn't telling us. I shuddered just thinking about it.

Mr. Gifford cracked the egg open and pulled out a scrap of paper. He read the clue Dunn had left for us. *"Look inside the biggest egg in the Aviary."*

Mr. Gifford scratched his head. "The biggest egg in the Aviary would have to be from the biggest bird, right? What's the biggest bird?"

"Oh no," I groaned. "The cassowary. They're carnivores. And they don't like people."

"Nothing in this place likes people," muttered Austin. "Except as chow."

Gramps pushed up his jacket sleeve and glanced at his watch. "Let's go. We don't know how many clues Dunn has left, and we have to find Megan and get out of here."

I knew a shortcut to the Aviary. I waved for everyone to follow me. We kept to the shadows, moving behind trees and buildings. A security guard rode by in a golf cart. The zoo was closed now. If the guard saw us, he'd make us leave. We stayed very still, squatting behind hedges until he disappeared. Finally we came to the Aviary. The cassowaries were kept in a special exhibit by themselves. We gathered around and peered in at them.

"I don't see any nests," said Austin. "Do they hide the eggs?"

"Maybe somebody will have to go in and check." Mr. Gifford sighed. "I guess I should do it. I can't let everyone else take all the risks." He looked at Gramps. "Should I become a gorilla for this?"

I put a hand on Mr. Gifford's arm. "Let's think about this a minute. Cassowaries will attack people. They'll attack anything that threatens their eggs."

"There aren't any eggs." Austin pointed to a sign. "These cassowaries are only a few months old."

We read the clue again. *Look inside the biggest egg in the Aviary.*

This was too hard. There were seventy species of birds in the Aviary. None were as big as the Cassowary, but some were at least two feet tall. Their eggs would be pretty large. There was another problem, too. The bigger birds were behind glass. How could we get to their eggs? How had Dunn gotten to their eggs? He wasn't even allowed in the zoo.

Gramps took charge. "Let's split up and fan out. Check your watches. We'll meet in back of the building in five minutes."

Gramps and Austin went one way, Mr. Gifford and I went the other. It was dark now. Mr. Gifford followed me through the front door of the Aviary. It was dark here, too. I'd visited this place a lot, so I knew where I was going.

"The birds are allowed to fly free in here, Mr. Gifford. The doorways are filled with long chains to keep them from escaping." I pushed the chains out of the way and let Mr. Gifford in. We stood in the Tropical Bird section.

Exotic trees and bushes abounded, and vines twined everywhere. Bright, colorful birds chirped and tweeted. A little creek wound through the jungle. Frogs and turtles hopped from logs, splashing into the water. I was too worried to enjoy it. I had to find the next clue.

We walked over a small bridge and through the chains to the next room. Several varieties of birds lived here, roosting on logs and tree branches. Their homes were protected by glass. They couldn't get out and people couldn't get in.

Then I spotted the egg. It was just beyond the door, in the hallway by the rear door. I called Mr. Gifford. Together, we went out to the hallway to look at it. The egg was huge, about four feet high. But it wasn't real. It was made of concrete. A hole in

111

one side allowed little kids to crawl inside and pretend to be baby birds.

"The clue must be inside the egg," said Mr. Gifford. He stepped toward the sculptured concrete.

"Wait," I said softly. "This is too easy. It might be a trap."

He didn't listen. He went right up to the egg and started to reach inside. Something rattled and hissed. Mr. Gifford jerked his hand away. Carefully, I looked inside. A rattlesnake was coiled in the bottom of the egg.

"Dunn must have put it there." I pointed to the burlap sack that lay on the floor next to the egg. "He probably stole it from the Reptile House when he took Megan."

"We have to get it out of there," said Mr. Gifford. "The clue is under the snake. I can see the paper."

Now we had another problem. We had to get the rattlesnake out of the concrete egg. We also had to take the snake back to the Reptile House. We couldn't just leave it where it could bite somebody. A child or elderly person could die from a rattlesnake bite.

When the rattling stopped, I peered at the snake again. What would lure the snake out of its hiding place? Food. Snakes eat mice and other small rodents. I knew where I could find some nice mice.

Gramps and Austin were waiting outside. I told them about the rattlesnake and what I was going to do. "Find some snake tongs," said Gramps.

I knew about snake tongs. They are long poles with pads on the end to protect the snake. I'd seen some in the back room of the Reptile House.

"I'll put the cattle prod back," I said. Gramps handed it to me.

I sprinted through the dark to the back door of the Reptile House. It was quiet. The light was out, so I knew Tim had gone for the night. I slipped inside and lay the cattle prod in the corner. Then I hurried to the freezer. Three bags of nice mice were right on top. A roll of string and a pair of scissors sat on Tim's workbench. I cut a couple of long pieces of string and shoved them in my pocket. The snake tongs hung from a hook near the door. Taking a bag of mice and the tongs, I hurried back to the Aviary.

Mr. Gifford opened the burlap bag and placed it next to the egg. I tied one end of the string around a mouse's neck. I signaled Mr. Gifford to move out of the way. My hands were shaking. I was very cold, and I was scared of rattlesnakes.

"Luke," Mr. Gifford whispered. "Let me help."

"Fine with me." I handed him the tongs.

"I'll lure him out," I said. "When he lands on the bag, grab his head with the tongs and hold him there. I'll pull the bag up around him. Ready?"

Mr. Gifford nodded. He held the end of the tongs near the bag. Gramps and Austin watched us from the doorway.

Moving slowly, I slid the mouse over the edge of the egg into view of the snake. I lowered the string, making the mouse dance. The snake's head rose up. It wove back and forth, watching the mouse. I eased the mouse over the side of the hole and let it go, onto the burlap sack. The snake followed it, oozing out of the egg and flopping down onto the sack.

Mr. Gifford was ready. He placed the tong's pads around the snake's head and held it firmly. I pulled up the sack and the snake dropped down into it.

Mr. Gifford took the bag from me. Holding it away from his body, he followed me to the Reptile House. Mr. Gifford placed the bag in an empty aquarium and quickly secured the lid over it. In a few seconds the snake slid out into the aquarium. He was home.

Gramps and Austin met us outside. They'd found the clue taped to the bottom of the egg. Austin read it to me.

"Look where the elephants put their feet."

113

Mr. Gifford took a deep breath. "The elephant compound has a large house for the elephants. It has a paddock, too. The elephants put their feet all over the place. How are we going to find the next clue?"

"We can't access any of the places where the elephants put their feet," said Austin.

Gramps spoke up. "Dunn can't get to them either." He scratched his chin. "If he morphed into a tiny, burrowing animal, he might be able to enter the elephant paddock."

Austin nodded. "Then one of us will morph into a tiny animal too. I'll do it."

Gramps held up a finger. "There's one more thing I forgot to tell you about this curse. I guess I'd better tell you now." I rolled my eyes. Austin laughed.

We gathered together in the men's restroom, trying to get warm. Gramps told us the last part of the curse.

He held up three fingers. "The curse only allows you to morph into an animal a total of three times. The fourth time you alter your form, you stay that way. So if you change into an animal a fourth time, you'll remain as that animal forever."

He pointed at Austin. "Austin changed into a bear during the first storm. Then, when we came back here today, he turned into an elephant and then a bear again. That's three times. He has no changes left."

Gramps nodded at me. "Luke has been a Komodo and a hippo. He started to morph into an eagle, but then stopped. He might have another change left. Then again, he might not."

I groaned. "What does that mean?"

"If growing feathers for three seconds meant you became an eagle, you have no more changes left. If you turn into an animal, you'll stay that way for the rest of your life. But you weren't fully changed to an eagle, so maybe you can become an animal one more time." He shrugged. "I just don't know. Of course it might mean that you can be three different animals. Maybe the number of times you change doesn't matter."

I slapped my forehead. "Yikes! How am I supposed to know what to do?"

Mr. Gifford held up the clue. "First, let's find Megan. I have two changes left. If we need somebody to transform, I'll do it."

He read the clue again. *"Look where the elephants put their feet."* He tucked the note into his shirt pocket. "Okay. Where do we start?"

We split into teams again. Austin went with Mr. Gifford to the Elephant House, and Gramps and I went to the elephants' paddock.

The paddock is like a big yard, with tall trees, and a small pond with lots of mud. An elephant was standing near the pond, sucking water into its trunk. Gramps and I slowly circled the outside of the enclosure, looking for possible hiding places. Bags filled with hay hung from the trees, so the elephants had to stretch their trunks up high to reach it. Those hay bags would be a good spot for a clue—unless an elephant ate it along with the hay.

On one side of the paddock was a wall with two openings about twelve inches in diameter. One was about three feet above the ground, and the other was about eight feet up.

Gramps pointed at them. "What are these for?"

"The upper one is for the vet to take blood samples from the area behind the elephant's ear. The elephants are trained to come up and stand there for the blood draw. Then they get a treat."

I pointed at the lower space. "Elephants need to have their feet trimmed, too. They're trained to put a foot into the hole. Then the keeper can trim their feet without going inside the paddock. It's safer that way."

"That's it!" said Gramps. *"Look where the elephants put their feet!"*

Remembering the rattlesnake, I warned Gramps. "Don't put your hand in."

"It's just a hole," said Gramps. "I can see right through it." He put his face close to the hole.

Something long and gray moved through the upper hole. It was an elephant's trunk. Gramps was busy looking into the lower space.

"Gramps!" I yelled. "Look out!"

A big spurt of water blasted Gramps' head. The long gray trunk slid back through the hole.

Gramps wiped water from his face and hair. He'd gotten wet in the rain, but now he was really soaked. "Blast that elephant," he grumbled. "Why did he do that?"

A loud sucking sound came from the pond. The elephant was getting more water.

I felt around the inside edge of the lower hole. The clue was in a plastic sandwich bag, taped to the top. I grabbed the bag and moved away just as another spurt of water rained through the top.

We hurried into the Elephant House. Mr. Gifford and Austin joined us.

I read the message aloud. Dunn had written, *"This is the last clue. The Death Adder is in a nest on top of the water tower."*

"On top of the water tower?" Austin's eyes widened. "How can we get her down?"

"Somebody's going to have to climb it," said Gramps. "That tower is pretty high. It's going to be dangerous in this rain. The ladder will be wet and slippery. It's made of metal, and it could be hit by lightning."

Austin yawned. "Maybe one of us could do it as an animal."

I shook my head. "It won't be you. You couldn't stay awake long enough to reach the top."

"Austin has used up all his changes anyway," said Gramps. "If he morphs into an animal again, he'll stay that way. I think."

116

As I stared up at the water tower, my heart began to pound. Who was going to climb that thing? Gramps couldn't do it, he was too old. Austin couldn't do it. He was too tired to do it as a human, and he'd used up his turns. Probably. Gramps didn't seem sure about that, but we couldn't take the chance.

Mr. Gifford was a gym teacher. Could he do it? He was kind of old, like Gramps. He probably couldn't do it as a gorilla. King Kong was the only gorilla I'd heard of that could climb that high, and he wasn't real.

That left me. As a human, I was terrified of heights. I'd already been a Komodo and a Hippo. If my three seconds of growing feathers counted as a morph, I didn't have any animal changes left, either.

Mr. Gifford stared up at the water tower. "She's my niece. I'll go up and get her."

"Turn into an animal that's a good climber," said Austin. "Maybe a monkey."

"Good idea." Mr. Gifford closed his eyes. He clenched his fists. He scrunched up his eyes and mouth until they were tightly closed. His face turned red. Nothing happened.

Finally he opened his eyes. He looked at his hands. They were still hands. He was still human.

He frowned. "Why didn't I become a monkey?"

Gramps shrugged. "Maybe you're a very distant cousin. Maybe you only got part of the curse."

"Then I'll have to climb it as a human," said Mr. Gifford. "Let's go."

"We'll take the car," said Gramps. "The water tower looks close, but it's over a mile away. We'll wait at the bottom. As soon as you get your niece, we're out of here."

Chapter Ten—Battle of the Tri-Morphs

Thunder rumbled in the distance. That was both good and bad. It was good because we needed the storm so Megan could change form. It was bad because metal conducts electricity. If Mr. Gifford was climbing the water tower when it was struck by lightning, he could be killed.

Gramps drove the car close to the water tower. He and I got out to cheer on Mr. Gifford. It was a long climb to the top. At least we could stand at the bottom and watch.

"Take my hat," said Gramps. "It will keep the water off your face." He handed Mr. Gifford his hat. Mr. Gifford clamped it on his head and started up. "Be careful, Roy," yelled Gramps.

At first Mr. Gifford climbed pretty fast. He put one hand and one foot up on a rung then followed with the other hand and foot. He kept going. Up twenty rungs. Then forty. Rain poured down on our faces as we stared up at him.

"Hang on tight, Roy," muttered Gramps. "Don't slip."

Finally Mr. Gifford was on the last section of ladder. He stepped off onto the walkway that circled the water tower. Now he had to find the nest and rescue Megan.

I narrowed my eyes, watching for something red. "I hope she doesn't bite him," I said. "By accident, I mean."

"I've got to sit down, Luke. You might as well get into the car, too. We're wet and cold. We'll be lucky if we don't get sick."

Gramps sat in the car and started the engine. I wanted to get in and warm up too, but I hated leaving Mr. Gifford out there all by himself. If he looked down, I wanted him to know someone was waiting for him. I wanted Megan to know that, too. She was probably lonely and scared after being up there by herself.

Then I saw Mr. Gifford waving from the top of the tower. He was starting down. I couldn't see Megan. He must have put her in his pocket.

Something small and red was falling through the air! It looked like a piece of red rope. But I knew what it was. It was Megan, the Death Adder. If she hit the ground from that height, the snake—and Megan—would die.

I made the decision before I even had time to think. In a nanosecond my body was covered with feathers. My wings lifted me up, up into the air. I swooped beneath her, opening my beak. I missed. A tiny shriek pierced the air as the snake plunged past me.

Soaring downward like a Kamikaze pilot, I swooped under her again. My beak was wide open for the catch. This time she landed in my beak safely. I yanked my head up to keep her from falling out. The "heads up" move took us both up into the air again. I circled, spiraling lower and lower. I slowed with each turn. Finally I landed and placed her gently on the ground.

Thunder rumbled and crashed overhead. Lightning shot across the sky. The little red snake shivered and began to roll in the dirt. Stretching, it blossomed into a dirty, bedraggled, red-headed girl. She jumped up and threw her arms around my neck.

"You saved my life, Luke! I thought I was going to die."

I had a neck! I knew, because Megan was still hanging onto it. I'd used up my last animal change, but I was a human again. Austin gave me a "thumbs up." I returned it.

Megan was still hanging on and crying. Gramps gently removed her.

"Sit in the car and get warm, Megan," said Gramps. "Your uncle is on his way down. He'll be here in a minute, and we'll all go home."

"I don't think so," snarled a voice behind us. Dunn Nikowski pointed his gun at us.

Gramps stepped out in front of us. "We had a deal, Dunn. We followed the clues and found her. The game is over now. You agreed to that."

"I lied." Dunn began to laugh. The cackling sound exploded into something long and low, like a hundred tires leaking air. The wind blew up around us, and the sky turned greenish-yellow. The air seemed to crackle with electricity. Goosebumps rose all over my body.

"Get in the car!" screamed Gramps. He threw me the keys. "Go somewhere safe. I'll handle this."

I couldn't move. The land had moved in front of me, forming a rope as thick as a trash can. The rope stretched and slithered, oozing across the ground and over the curb of the parking lot. Black eyes bugged from its head. An incredibly humongous snake! On the back of the snake's head were two round circles, one on each end of a "U"-shaped mark. Dunn had morphed into the deadly, spectacled cobra. The cobra was longer than two train cars. It could spew enough venom to kill every person in a major city.

The snake's body bent and slid, doubling over itself to form a figure-eight. Then it coiled again, spreading out next to me. It reared up, swaying back and forth over my head. Its hood widened, flaring out four feet in each direction. Eyes bigger than truck tires glared down at me. Any second it would open its mouth and swallow me whole.

Suddenly a great cloud of dust swirled into the air, forming a weasel-shaped mass. The shape ballooned into a giant mongoose, as big as a Tyrannosaurus Rex. It circled the cobra on slender legs. We were saved. A mongoose could kill a cobra. But where had the mongoose come from?

"Austin!" I cried.

"I'm right here." He was standing next to me, watching with his mouth open.

"Is that Mr. Gifford?"

Mr. Gifford was still climbing down the ladder. Megan was in the car. There was only one person missing. Gramps!

Gramps had morphed into a mongoose? I couldn't believe it. He'd told Austin and me about the curse, but he never told us it affected him, too. Now he'd transformed himself to save my life. I hoped he hadn't used up all his animal changes when he was young.

The cobra turned away from us, following the dance of the mongoose. Suddenly it struck, darting at the mongoose in a blur of speed. It missed. Retreating, the cobra turned again, slithering into striking distance.

The mongoose danced sideways, teasing it. The cobra coiled, flared its hood and struck again. Again it missed.

I licked my lips. I wanted to back away. Gramps had told me to get into the car, but I couldn't move.

The cobra's head swayed back and forth. It stretched and flattened out its hood. It struck fiercely, as if it wanted to swallow the mongoose. The mongoose leapt just in time, flying above the cobra's strike zone. It landed on its feet, just out of reach. The cobra hissed and shot forward again. The mongoose leapt again, landing atop the cobra and sinking its razor-sharp teeth into the cobra's head. The snake's body quivered and rolled, trying to free itself from the mongoose's death-grip. The battle was almost over. Or so I thought.

The snake's tail began to grow, blowing up like a car-sized balloon. Dunn was altering form again. The snake kept growing, first one way and then another, into another shape. Was it a big cat? A dog? It was so huge I couldn't tell. Then I saw the spots on its fur, and the shape of its head. It was a hyena. As the hyena's head formed, the mongoose lost its grip and rolled over backwards.

The hyena had grown to the size of a long, two-story house. Its bark roared across the parking lot, like a thousand people laughing. Globs of drool dripped from its mouth. A hyena's bite could lop off a human head. What could it do to the mongoose? Did Gramps have any more animal shapes left? If he didn't, we were all done for. If he could morph again, what animal could take a hyena? Then I remembered.

I shouted out to him. "Gramps! A wolverine! I think a wolverine could take him!" Mr. Gifford ran up. He grabbed my arm and pulled me away.

The mongoose curled up into a ball and rolled away from the hyena. As it tumbled, it twisted and grew into another ginormous animal. Its long snout became a stubby nose. The smooth pelt sprouted long, chocolate-brown fur. Patches of white fur appeared over the animal's eyes and chest. Its thin legs grew thick with muscle. Each leg ended in a wide paw with deadly sharp claws. Though it was bigger than a truck, it was much smaller than the hyena. That didn't matter. Gramps had become something even more vicious than a hyena. He'd changed into a giant wolverine!

The hyena snarled and drooled, backing away. The wolverine sprang at the hyena's back leg. The hyena kicked, turning fast, trying to grab the wolverine with its teeth. The wolverine dropped back, crouching for another pounce. It sprang at the hyena and sliced into its rear quarter. The wolverine's razor-sharp claws cut through the hyena's fur. A trail of blood dripped across the parking lot. The hyena whirled, trying to kick the wolverine off its back. Snapping, it tried to clamp its jaws onto the wolverine's leg. The wolverine dropped to the ground and circled again.

Puddles of saliva dripped from the hyena's mouth. It pounced, but once again the wolverine moved out of reach. They repeated the deadly dance. Circle. Attack. Fall back. Each time they got closer, snapping and clawing as if to eat the other alive. At last the hyena flopped to the ground, rolling away from the wolverine. Was he giving up? Was it over? Or was Dunn going to morph again?

The hyena suddenly leapt into the air and sprang, jaws wide open. The wolverine rolled sideways and grabbed the hyena's hindquarter as he flew past. The gleaming talons raked across the hyena's belly, drawing a new river of blood. The hyena shrieked and fell to the ground. It rolled out to the middle of the parking lot and melted, spreading out into a pond of gray scales. It was changing again.

The wolverine was panting. Gramps was too old for this. If only I could help him. But if I morphed again, that would be it for me. No matter what I became, I'd stay that way forever.

The earth started to shake and a strange noise filled the air. It sounded as if a herd of elephants was crossing the parking lot. I wheeled around and gasped in horror. A monster crocodile waddled toward us, eyes glowing like yellow fire. The head was as large as a semi, and the body was the length of four semis hooked together. The croc's heavy jaws opened, showing jagged teeth. Every one of those teeth was bigger than me. The crocodile bellowed. The sound knocked me down. I shoved myself backward, trying to get out of his reach. I couldn't move fast enough. He'd eat me or crush me. Either way, I was going to die.

Thunder exploded behind me. A hippopotamus, big as a three-story building, plowed past me. It scraped one huge foot against the pavement, like a bull does when it's ready to charge.

The crocodile clamped his huge jaws down on the hippo's leg. Then the croc rolled, pulling the hippo's leg out from under him. The hippo crashed to the ground, splintering the pavement. The hippo whipped its massive head to the side and bit the croc's belly. The croc let go of the hippo and flipped to the side. It snapped its jaws, ready to bite.

My fists were clenched at my side, and my heart was pounding. Gramps couldn't keep this up much longer. Austin got out of the car. He stood next to me, watching the fight.

"What if he can't take the croc?" asked Austin. He sounded scared.

"We'll have to help."

"How? What could we do?"

I glanced away from the fight long enough to meet his eyes. "Another hippo. That was Dunn's fourth change. If we can kill him, he's gone."

"It would be the same for us," said Austin. "It will be our fourth change too. If we take another shape, we'll stay that way forever."

I eyed him steadily. "We can't let Gramps die."

"No."

Austin was smart. He had a lot to give to the world. I couldn't let him be a hippopotamus for the rest of his life.

"I'm the oldest. I'll do it."

"Maybe neither one of us will need to do it."

The crocodile was fighting with all of his might. He whipped his tail across the parking lot, knocking three cars into the air. Then he rolled over, flattening seven more cars and leaving a trail of metal trash. The Gramps hippo opened his jaws and bit the crocodile's tail. The croc howled and rolled again, but his tail didn't go with him. It lay on the pavement, ragged and bleeding.

125

The croc's eyes flared, shooting darts of fire. The hippo wheeled to the side, opening his huge mouth. His dagger-like teeth came down on the croc, severing it in half. The croc melted to the pavement, like a balloon that's been pierced and lost its air. I waited, afraid to breathe. Would the crocodile morph into another animal?

Seconds passed. Nothing happened. The croc was dead. Dunn Nikowski was dead. Gramps was back to his own human self. He sat on the pavement, trying to catch his breath.

People were coming. Though we were over a mile away, they'd heard the noise from the last battle. Gramps' car screeched to a halt next to us, Mr. Gifford at the wheel.

"Get in!" yelled Mr. Gifford.

Austin and I helped Gramps up and into the car. We pulled away. From the rear window I saw the DART team crossing the parking lot. They were all carrying tranquilizer guns. I laughed. Those guns would be useless against the tri-morphs. It didn't matter, though. Thanks to Gramps, Dunn was gone.

Chapter Eleven—Home Sweet Home

We dropped off Mr. Gifford and Megan at his house. Megan put her arms around my neck and hugged me. It was really embarrassing. She started to hug Austin, then stepped back and shook his hand. Mr. Gifford shook hands with everyone. At last Gramps headed the car toward home.

"Your parents will be back tomorrow," said Gramps. "I don't think we should tell them about any of this, do you?"

"No!" Austin and I said together. They wouldn't believe it, and it would only make them worry.

The sun came up just as we pulled into the driveway.

"I'm hungry," said Austin. "I'd like a peanut butter and jelly sandwich and some cocoa with marshmallows."

"Want me to make a fire?" Gramps put his hands on his hips and looked at me. "Are you cold?"

"Nope. Just hungry." I grinned at him. "How do you feel, Gramps? Are you tired? Do you hurt anywhere? That croc got your leg pretty good."

Gramps rolled up his trouser. There were a couple of scratches on his leg, but they didn't look deep. "I'm fine." He put his arms up and flexed his muscles. "I feel twenty years younger."

"I feel twenty years older," I muttered.

"Let's take it easy for a while, and then we should clean things up around here. I don't want your folks to think I let you run wild."

Austin and I laughed.

"But we did run wild, Gramps," I said. "Really, really crazy-wild. And so did you."

We were quiet for a minute. Austin and I looked at each other, and Austin nodded. We both had questions about what happened at the water tower. In my mind, I could still picture those gigantic creatures battling each other. It was hard to believe one of those animals was now at the stove, cooking bacon.

I licked my lips. What if he wouldn't tell us? Maybe it was one of those grown-up things kids never find out about until fifty years later, when it's too late.

"Gramps, have you told us everything about this curse? You explained how it started, with Dunn killing the Komodo. You didn't say that you and Dunn could change into animals, too."

Austin asked, "Will we pass it on? If we have children, will they have it, too?"

Gramps pressed the button on the coffee machine and the black stuff poured out into a mug. He stirred in cream. He was taking his time. Finally, turning off the stove, he sat down across the table from us.

"I told you that when we were in the Navy, Dunn and I went to Komodo Island. There were Komodos everywhere. The Komodo I killed to save Dunn's life was very special. It was a rare, pink Komodo. It lived in a cave we were told was off-limits to us. People brought the Komodo food. They believed if the pink Komodo was happy, their lives would be happy, too.

"Dunn went into the cave. The Komodo was asleep. He poked it with a stick a couple of times. The Komodo woke up and bit him. It wouldn't let go of Dunn's leg, and I had to shoot it.

Dunn was losing a lot of blood. I put a tourniquet around his leg to stop the bleeding. I took him to the hospital in the jeep. His leg was injured so badly they had to amputate part of it. That's where we left off with the story, right?"

"You told us a medicine woman came into his hospital room and placed a necklace around his neck," said Austin.

"That's right. Hanging from the necklace was a shell picturing a Komodo dragon. There was one other thing I left out. The medicine woman's daughter was with her. She tried to get the medicine woman to stop talking and leave the room. But the medicine woman wouldn't go. She placed the necklace around Dunn's neck and spoke to him. Then she waved her stick over him and me and spoke more words. I didn't understand any of it."

Gramps sipped his coffee. "My leave was over and I had to get back to the ship. It was anchored about a mile off shore, in deep water. Smaller boats were waiting on the shore to take us. While I was waiting my turn, I saw the medicine woman's daughter again. She spoke English, so I asked her to tell me what was said."

Austin and I leaned in closer. Gramps continued the story.

"This is what the daughter of the medicine woman told me. `My mother gave you and your friend a blessing. She gave your friend the strength of the Komodo to help him heal. She gave you the strength of the Komodo, too. She said you would each have the strength of three other wild creatures to help you. She did this so the two of you could find another pink Komodo and return it to our people. If you return it, our people will be happy again. If you do not return the pink Komodo, the blessing will become a curse. You, your children and their children will become the wild creatures you choose to embody."

Austin and I looked at each other. It was so quiet I could hear the ticking clock in the other room.

I licked my lips. "So, if Austin and I ever have children, they could become zoo animals too?"

Gramps' shoulders drooped. He looked very tired. "I'm afraid so. She told me the curse would be passed down from us to our children and grandchildren. It wouldn't stop until another pink Komodo was returned to them. She told me where I could find one, but my leave was over and I couldn't stay on Komodo Island." Gramps sat up straight, and his voice became stronger. "I was in the U.S. Navy, for heaven's sake. I had to get back to my ship." He waved his hand in the air. "I couldn't just take off and go hunting for Komodo dragons. Besides, I didn't believe in curses. The nurse told me the medicine woman was just a harmless old lady who hung around the hospital. I thought the whole thing was nonsense."

We were quiet for a few minutes. I thought about the storm that turned the sky weird colors. I was a Komodo dragon and Austin had become a bear. When we went back to the zoo the second time, we'd become other animals. Gramps and Dunn had been enormous creatures. Was something else going to happen to us? Had Gramps told us everything?

"Did she tell you anything more?" I asked. "Like how the curse would take place?"

Gramps shrugged. "The medicine woman told me that when the Komodo died, his strength passed into us and we would become like him. It happened to you two, but it never happened to me until today. I doubt it ever affected Dunn before he changed today."

He went on. "Though it never occurred, I feared that it might. When I left the Navy, I studied quantum physics. I tried to learn whether a human could change into an animal. I thought I had it figured out. I thought the energy in our bodies could be altered by disrupting the magnetic field. Now I'm not so sure."

"Some native American tribes believe in shape-shifters," I said. "Maybe it's something like that."

"Maybe." He rubbed his hands together. "That's enough talk about the curse. What are we having for breakfast?"

We had eggs, bacon, pancakes and frozer
Austin and I each ate a chocolate bar for dessert.

Gramps took a nap. Austin and I kept checking on hu.
make sure he was okay. Austin even took his pulse. While
Gramps slept, we showered, brushed our teeth and changed
into clean clothes. By that time we were hungry again. We made
peanut butter and jelly sandwiches and hot cocoa and ate in
front of the television.

"This tastes good," said Austin. "How does it taste to you?"

"Perfect. I haven't had a hankering for nice mice since we
got home. How about you? Are you still sleepy?"

Austin pushed his plate aside and stretched. "I'm tired, but
not like I was before. I just want to sleep through the night. I
don't want to hibernate until spring." We laughed. It felt good to
be together again.

"I'm not cold anymore, either." I said. "It's wonderful to be
warm again."

Austin eyed me. "Do you think it's really over? Our animal
traits are really gone?"

I thought for a minute. I wasn't sure. I kept thinking of when
I almost changed into an eagle. I had stopped myself and didn't
transform completely. That worried me a little. But I wasn't a
Komodo anymore, or any other reptile. I wasn't cold. I didn't
feel like eating any nice mice, or putting them on my cereal. All I
wanted was my soft, warm bed. And maybe some fresh air.

"There's something I didn't tell Gramps," said Austin. "He
said the medicine woman put a necklace on Dunn's neck."

"Right. A necklace with a Komodo painted on a shell."

"Here's the thing," said Austin. "I've seen that necklace."

"What?" I put my cocoa down and stared at him. "Where?"

"A girl at school was wearing it. A girl in my class."

"Megan Gifford?"

He nodded. "Yes. How did you know?"

se of the Komodo

"Because she went through all that we did at the zoo with her uncle. They're part of this. We just don't know where they fit in, or why."

Austin held up his hands. "How would the shell necklace get from Dunn Nikowski to Megan Gifford?"

"Who knows? Why did Megan turn into a Death Adder? Why did Roy Gifford change into a Silverback?" I had more questions than answers.

"Let's think about this a minute," said Austin. "Both of us became animals. Mr. Gifford and Megan morphed into animals. Then Gramps changed, and Dunn Nikowski did, too.

"The medicine woman gave Dunn the necklace," added Austin. "Fifty years later it shows up on Megan Gifford."

We were quiet for several seconds. Then we looked at each other and smiled. The answer was so clear. We said it at the same time. "They're related to Dunn Nikowski."

"Mr. Gifford will have to research his family tree," said Austin. "Dunn will be there somewhere."

I didn't like the idea of Megan and her uncle being related to someone like Dunn Nikowski. They were kind and nice. Dunn Nikowski was mean. Worse than mean.

"I'm not sure we should ask any more questions," I said. "We might not like the answers."

"When I see Megan, I'm going to ask her to bring that necklace over so we can examine it." Austin picked up his dishes and took them to the kitchen. I picked up my dishes and followed him.

Austin loaded the dishwasher and I wiped down the counters. I was thirsty, so I turned on the tap and ran water into a glass. It was good to drink from a glass again.

We checked on Gramps. He was sleeping soundly, so we went upstairs to play on our computers. My room was clean and quiet. The carpet felt soft under my feet. Everything seemed beautiful and clean and warm.

132

When Gramps woke up, we did laundry, vacuumed the floors and cleaned the bathrooms. We didn't want Mom and Dad to think we lived like wild animals while they were gone.

Finally it was bedtime. As I lifted my arms to pull off my shirt, I saw something white. The white stuff was soft. I moved closer to the mirror to get a good look. There were feathers. Tiny, white feathers. This was what happened at the zoo, too, earlier. I had sprouted feathers on my arms before I stopped myself from changing the rest of the way. Now here they were, back again. But only about ten percent of my body had feathers. That would leave me ninety-percent human. That wasn't so bad, was it?

I felt fine. I liked human food. My life was normal. A few feathers wouldn't keep me from getting an education or leading a happy life.

When I went to bed, I fixed my pillows and blankets in a cozy little circle and nestled down. I didn't tell Austin or Gramps about the feathers. There was nothing they could do about it, and there was no point in worrying them. I could wear a tee-shirt when I went swimming. I'd just say I didn't want to get sunburned. Maybe one of these days I'd get Gramps to take us to the nature preserve. They had a couple of Eagle nests there. The nests were up pretty high, so we'd need binoculars. I was interested in learning all about them.

I also decided to continue in Scouting. I would earn all the merit badges that had to do with science, or nature, or animals. Maybe I'd even become an Eagle Scout.

Austin and I might have disagreements in the future, but we'd never fight again. We'd been through some trying times in the zoo. I'd never forget how hungry he was, and how hard it was to find food for him. Knowing my brother was hungry was the worst part of our awful adventure.

I remembered something else, too. My brother had said he wanted to be like me. He got better grades and was better at sports, but he still looked up to me. Because of those three terrible days, we were close in a way we'd never been before. Austin had saved my life and I'd saved his. I didn't need to fear he'd be bullied or shoved into his locker. He could handle whatever came his way. I had his back, and he had mine. Together, we could face anything.

The End

About the Author

M.C. (Peg) Berkhousen wrote her first poem in sixth grade and has been writing all her life. She was raised in Three Rivers, Michigan, a rural Midwestern town where she frequently visited the library and checked out Cherry Ames and Sue Barton nursing stories.

After graduation from Borgess School of Nursing in Kalamazoo, Michigan, Peg continued to write about her nursing experiences. She won Michigan Nurse Writer of the Year for her story about using journalism therapy with a psychiatric patient who was aboard the USS Hornet when it was sunk by the Japanese during WWII.

While working in Staff Development at St. Joseph Mercy Hospital, Pontiac, Michigan, she wrote, produced and directed staff training videos that were published by J.B. Lippincott, New York. She wrote the script and was Associate Producer for "Lincoln...In His Own Words," a project for Lincoln Life

Insurance Company, narrated by actor Hal Holbrook. On faculty for Trinity International Health Services, Peg provided Management Training and Consultation to Franciscan Sisters at Matre Dei Hospital, Bulawayo, Zimbabwe, Africa. She ended her nursing career as Director of Clinical Services, Trinity Home Health Services, and is now writing full time.

Curse of the Komodo, targeted to children in grades 6th through 8th, is her first published novel. The second two books of the Komodo trilogy, *90% Human*, and *Return to Komodo Island*, are planned for publication in 2018. Peg resides in Ottawa Hills, Ohio. She hopes to continue volunteering at the amazing Toledo Zoo, where she once interviewed a visiting Komodo dragon.

Hope you enjoy
There are two
more in the
trilogy

Love,

Maurie
2017

CPSIA information can be obtained
at www.ICGtesting.com
Printed in the USA
FFOW05n0552030817